At Scales Edge

Part One

Copyright 2020 S.M. Winter
Published by S.M. Winter

I0618544

S.M. Winter
Publishing

Smashwords Edition License Notes

To the future.

Acknowledgements

First, I would like to thank my Beta Readers. Without whom I would not have been able to publish this novel. I appreciate their unfiltered feedback that always brings my writing to the next level. Not to mention more rum in my glass. Megan, Christy, Kane, Nicole, Marc, and Paul; Thank you.

I would also like to thank my editor, Aimee, who has to deal with me on a daily basis on rewrites. She's very patient and I love her dearly, even when she reads me my own writing in a voice made for horror movies… or romantic comedies.

Finally, I want to thank the readers. Especially the women. Your experiences, while unique to you, follow a pattern of societal misogyny which we've all lived through our entire lives. You are powerful, even though there are some who seek to steal that power from you. It needs to change.

I will also state that no, I don't think the systematic subjugation of men is the answer… but it might be fun.

Enjoy.

The following is an adult novel with the following possible triggers: sexual assault, sex, strong language, gaslighting, brainwashing, non-consent.

An explosion rocked me back onto my heels.

If I hadn't been expecting it, I would be on the ground like the others.

But this wasn't my first rodeo.

"Advance!" I yelled at the greenies as they ducked and covered.

The heat was immense. I watched one soldier pick herself up, grit her teeth and keep moving. Tears were streaming down her face, tracking dirty streaks down her cheeks and neck.

Her legs wobbled, but she remained low as she advanced at the front of the group. I could see her fear and admired the way she pushed through it. She was one to watch.

Blast helmets gleamed in the light of the fires ahead. Vehicles exploded. A building collapsed. I remained watchful, even though I knew this simulation like the back of my hand. You'd never know when someone would throw you a curveball.

I pressed forward from our flank as they moved up the street. They weren't in the formation they'd learned recently, but I held my tongue. This was just a test simulation to see who stood out and remembered their training.

As they moved, I noted two soldiers flanking the one I'd seen earlier. They crouched as they moved swiftly but cautiously toward the checkpoint.

With a rallying yell, men came at the recruits from all sides. I side stepped a rushing man and moved into the shadows so that I could observe the chaos. Some held crude weapons as they charged, others tossed flaming cocktails, their explosions adding to the growing chaos. . One soldier took a knife to the back as she was distracted by everything happening in front of her. She fell and the man moved on as her image wavered and disappeared.

After several minutes, the three I'd initially noted were

the only ones left. They stood back to back with their rifles held high, conserving their dwindling ammo as much as possible. They lined up shots and put the enemy down quickly and efficiently.

I saw the smiles of triumph on their faces as the last man fell. All three immediately looked to me, an arrogant air of victory surrounding them. That was their mistake.

With a screeching whistle, the three were thrown apart like rag dolls.

A lone woman she stood in the middle of the road ahead, focused on reloading the RPG she held. They hadn't noticed her. The greenies had been so focused on annihilating the men surrounding them, that they'd forgotten to look ahead.

In the time it took them to look at me with arrogance, so sure in their victory, she was able to line up her shot and let loose an RPG. Before she could fire again I smirked at them.

"End simulation," I sighed.

"That wasn't fair!" The leader of the three stomped toward me, ripping off her AV glasses and pointing a finger at my chest.

"I didn't design the simulation," I quirked a brow as she rose on her toes to meet me eye to eye.

She was careful not to touch me. Her posture was threatening, nonetheless.

"Rhonda," one of the flankers whispered.

"No," she waved the flanker off. I noted that the third was at her side as well, unconsciously moving into the defensive.

"Careful, recruit," I cautioned. I didn't move a muscle as the others in the class turned to watch the show. They knew what could happen to a recruit who threatened their superior.

"You just didn't want us to surpass your record," the girl snapped into my chest. It was the closest she could reach, as I stood nearly two heads above her.

I smiled as she began to gesture toward the screen, giving me an opening.

"A lesson you must always remember," quick as a snake I

snagged her wrist, and using the momentum of my turn, I pulled her over my shoulder so she tumbled over me and landed on her back. This happened so fast that the flankers just stood there watching, slack-jawed. I continued to hold her wrist and planted a booted foot against her neck lightly, but firmly, as she struggled to regain the breath.

I let the silence hang heavy in the room for another beat.

"Even women can join the resistance. Always be on your guard, or you will be lucky to only end up with a boot on your neck."

I released my hold and walked to the wall of silicone busts designed to hold the equipment the class had been using. I refused to let my superiors know that they creeped me out with their absent staring eyes, and blue-clear gel skin.

I placed my AV glasses and sensor gloves in their designated places next to the bust that held my personal equipment. The greenies in the room stepped around the girl on the ground silently as she lay there, her breath slowly returning to normal. One of the flankers extended a hand but she shoved it away and got up to follow the rest of the class. I moved to the door and watched them put their equipment away the same way I had. There were a few whispers of "Thank you Hop" and "I can't wait for next time" as they left. I nodded and held myself at parade rest as they filtered out.

"She really is as tough as they say," I heard one of the flankers whisper as the last three left. As they filtered down the hall, I even heard a few reverent *Zeros*. I shook my head, with a small self-indulgent grin and turned back to the task at hand. It was amazing that such a small nickname could still be uttered nearly twenty years later.

Powering down the machine, I ensured that the equipment was all accounted for. I noted the recruits who had left their helmets hanging messily off the busts. They would start out with negative points during the next class. When I was sure that everything was ship-shape I walked out into the hall, closing the door behind me to the simulation room. The locks engaged and I stood, absorbing the late afternoon light that shone through the wall of windows opposite the classrooms.

The building, and others like it, had been created early in the 22nd century, to be seen as a beacon of light and hope. There were only ten in the entire world, one in every territory on Earth. The reflection of the light in the entirely glass outer walls was to symbolize the new beginning for Earth under leadership that would preserve the planet, and a new way of rule focused on the planet and human sustenance rather than money and materialistic gains. It seemed an impossible task when our foremothers took up the reigns but they'd succeeded; bringing the world back from the brink of destruction, and our race with it. The Universal World Government Authority College was created, a completely free institution that fed both physical and mental aspects of learning. It was completely uniform in what was tested and taught so that every student, regardless of background, would get the exact same education as anyone else. Because of this, the UWGA and its colleges were termed the Uniformity.

I stretched, rolling my neck on my shoulders, and finally let my body relax. If that was the best the Uniformity had to offer, then my record would be safe for another year.

It always surprised me when the recruits who came through here didn't believe that a woman could betray everything we had created. I shook my head and strode down the glowing hallway to take advantage of the ten minutes between classes to relieve myself. I was back standing at parade rest again when the next set of recruits entered.

"Grab the first available set of VR equipment and take your station," I barked.

Their initial hesitance melted away as they rushed to grab their equipment and then to the round raised platforms, arranged in rows of three back and five across. Mine stood front and center, facing the others. I slipped on my gloves, which tracked my movements, then the glasses. They curled around the ear and had noise canceling earbuds attached.

"Suit-up!" I barked and stepped up onto the platform.

The front of the platform had a chest tall handrail, with the base consisting of a circular tread that moved in sync with your every step. It sat two meters in circumference to compensate for anyone who ended up prone, which they all did at some point. It cut down on the amount of recruits in each class, but that meant I was able to pay special attention to those under my training.

As soon as I stepped onto the platform it began to glow and an administrative menu popped up, hovering in midair for me to see.

Hoplomachos 5-B Casey: Training program 5A : Initiate?

"Verify comms," I said quietly, so that only those who had their glasses on and secured could hear.

Every recruit signalled active. I stood at parade rest, just watching. I could see the heart rates of those around me through the administrative menu and waited. Some began to slow, others raced with the uncertainty. Recruits began looking around, as if curious what we were waiting for. There were a few who were crouched inready positions, and stayed that way. My lips twitched towards a smile, it was obvious that they assumed it would be the same simulation the last class had gone through.

"Harness up!" I barked.

I reached up and attached the harness hanging above my head to the link on my standard issue utility belt. I saw confusion then compliance as they mimicked my actions. From the projected menu, I used hand signals to load the program I wanted for this class. Their heartbeats began to spike as they realized that the program may not be the same as what the last class experienced. When I had the program loaded and ready, I stood still and waited for all of the recruits to relax again.

As soon as all of their heart rates had calmed to a rested rate, I pushed the button to initiate the program.

The scenery loaded around me. This one was one of my favorites. I stood on a small floating platform, in the middle of a large placid lake. Bright green trees surrounded the shores. A large yellow sun in a cornflower blue sky arched high above. The humidity immediately had my shirt sticking to my chest as I stood above the recruits, who sat in three rafts. Each raft contained five recruits. Two on either side and one at the aft for steering.

"Paddles!" I barked and they picked up their lightweight paddles, holding them at the ready.

A few of the soldiers began giggling. I wasn't sure if it was in relief or anticipation.

"North face!" I commanded, and the three rafts turned to the north efficiently.

"Forward, Paddle!"

Quickly and quietly the three rafts moved forward as one. Soon, as I expected, the company began to race. They'd already forgotten that this was a battle simulation and were trying to pull ahead of one another, lost in the simple joy of boating. This would be an important lesson.

As one recruit crowed her triumph at pulling ahead of the other two rafts, she suddenly slumped forward, dropping her paddle. Her form shook, then disappeared.

A zipping sound became noticeable as another, then another, recruit went down. One recruit panicked and stood up in their raft.

ZIP... ZIP ZIP.

The one standing took three hits to the chest and fell into the water.

The rest of the recruits finally realized what was happening. Some abandoned the rafts and attempted to swim ashore, but were picked off one by one. Soon enough there were only two left. They'd managed to overturn one of the abandoned rafts and were using it as a shield. It offered some cover, but the rubber raft was heavy and not bulletproof. The enemy sprayed the raft and eventually their bullets hit their marks. I double checked my administrative menu, confirming that all recruits had fallen.

I disengaged the program and watched the crestfallen recruits wait for their impending verbal lashing.

"I would be disappointed, if this wasn't exactly what I expected," was all I said.

Heads drooping, the recruits moved to the wall and replaced their equipment. When they were finished, I looked at the clock, which logged that only 15 minutes lapsed. They formed neat rows, standing at attention, waiting for me to dismiss them. I replaced my equipment and returned to the head of the class where I stood at attention, facing them and staring over their shoulders.

When I did not dismiss them immediately I could feel the confusion and I waited for the first person to break. I saw one head shift slightly to look at another recruit.

"Ah Ten Huh!" I commanded, and their backs snapped straight again. The recruit immediately faced forward.

"Dismissing you early would be a reward," I barked at them. "You will stand at attention until the bell rings and wait for your dismissal."

I studied them as I made the announcement. Not so much as a flicker.

Good, I nodded mentally.

I stood perfectly still while watching them intently. There was a reason I was not-so-lovingly referred to as *Sidewinder zero*.

One particularly forward recruit once told me they could hear the rattle once. As if the tension and quiet had its own sound. I knew the perception, and did nothing to change it. I didn't mind the fact that I was left to my own devices more often than not, as people avoided me. The Sidewinder had been added later in my career when people realized I was incredibly hard to read except when I was displeased. Even though my facial expression and posture wouldn't change, there was a shift in the air when someone challenged me.

The Zero part was a longer story, and one I didn't especially like thinking about.

A dark aspect of my initiation into the Uniformity.

"Ah Ten Huh!" I shouted as eyes darted to clock over my head.

My internal clock said there was thirty five minutes left, these recruits needed to learn how to tell time without a wall device.

The time passed slowly for them as they twitched and shifted, and I was forced to call them to attention again and again. Finally the bell rang, and I watched them all relax.

"Ah Ten Huh!" I startled them and they snapped back to attention. "I did not dismiss you, you will wait for my command."

Sweat dripped down their brows as they waited.

"Dismissed!" I shouted and they all scattered.

I shook my head as they left.

"Hopeless," a familiar voice came from the doorway.

My head snapped up at the sound.

"Well, Victoria," I shrugged as I once again righted the equipment to prepare for the next class. "That's what you get when you recruit based on name and not ability."

"I was talking about you," Victoria leaned against the doorway and smirked.

I continued moving about the room, ignoring her jibe. I knew she would explain it without asking. She flipped her long, straight black hair that fell below her waist. It gleamed with the light at her back. I used to envy her ability to look gorgeous in every situation. Now I just wished she'd disappear.

"Always the same. It's an antique." Victoria sniffed as she stepped into the room to survey her surroundings. "Dropping the greenies into random simulations to edge out who's got good instincts and who show leadership qualities."

"True," I stood with my back to the room, but I listened. "Though, sometimes, someone reprograms a SIM to... surprise me."

"Noticed that did you?" Victoria whispered, close.

I knew that she wanted me to react, so I moved slowly and efficiently as I finished closing up the classroom. I didn't need to answer, because I'd known she had been the one to tamper with my SIMs. I wondered, as I had a million times since we'd broken up, what I'd ever seen in her. Victoria was a beautiful woman, of that there was no doubt. Without looking, I could still describe her perfectly.

Skin the color of roasted almonds, with eyes the same shape but not the same hue. The color of her eyes was much, much darker. Nearly black, and almost as unreadable as my own. At one time, I would have enjoyed sparing verbally with this woman. Now I was just tired. Victoria knew that I could, and in fact had, best her in nearly every competition and test of proficiency. However, because of this, she was hell bent on making my life miserable.

"Aww," Victoria smirked as I turned. "I thought you liked surprises."

I didn't and don't. It's why I make it my business to always know what's happening around me, and more importantly, why it's happening, but she knew that.

"Did the Grunt complain?" I asked calmly.

"Oh, you're no fun anymore," Victoria pouted prettily. "Nothing but work talk, Casandra. You need to lighten up. Our trials are over."

Maybe for you. I knew better than to answer so I just tilted my head and watched her, waiting for her to get to the point.

"Alright," Victoria relented. "Of course she complained. You assaulted her."

"She challenged her direct superior and made threatening hand gestures in full view of the entire company in attendance," I shrugged. "We endured worse."

"Of course we did," Victoria huffed and crossed her arms. "Because we were surrounded by a bunch of sticks-in-the-mud, just like you're turning out to be."

I could tell my lack of empathy was digging under her skin.

"I produce exemplary soldiers," I stated. "Is there an official complaint against me?"

"No," Victoria sighed deeply as if genuinely disappointed. "But you do need to tread carefully in the future with her, if you want to keep it that way."

"My record is unimpeachable."

"Just call this a friendly warning from the Dean of Admissions," Victoria trotted toward the door. "It's yours to take or leave."

And with that, thankfully, she left.

I finished locking the equipment and then moved to the doorway myself. Locking the door behind me, I looked down the empty hallway and contemplated the evening ahead. My lack of weekend plans stretched ahead of me and I smiled for the first time in hours. There was only one thing left to do before heading home.

I walked swiftly down the empty corridor by closed classroom doors. When a class was in session, or finished, the doors were to remain shut. Practical procedures employed by the Uniformity. Even though every inch of the school was under surveillance, it was best just to create a routine to avoid forgetting any of the policies enforced.

A voice broke through the pressing quiet as I approached the last doorway before the stairs, leading to the first floor and my exit. The door was left cracked open, as they were expecting me. I slipped in to observe, as all teachers were required to do that worked for the Uniformity's College program. We followed a tight schedule to reinforce the Scholastic Board's approved uniform lectures. As a teacher, we were allowed the freedom to enhance the material to our own style but the tests would all be the same, so the coursework would need to fall in line.

"...and though The Scourge was an awful event that ended in so many deaths, the Goddess saw the need for the world to change. And so it has. Since Men were removed from power we have made leaps and bounds in Science, and now enjoy an unparalleled peace and prosperity that this world has never before seen."

I shut the door behind me quietly and took a seat at the back of the lecture hall. Historia was one of the few classes that was allowed a larger lecture room. There were about 100 seats in all. I pulled out a small notebook and began taking notes. The use of the Goddess needed to be put into context, so I waited for the professor to continue. I noted a few of the students were snoozing in their seats.

"Though I tend to color my teachings with the Word of the Goddess," the professor continued. "I use only facts in my teachings. Because this is not a World Religions class, no religious questions will be on the tests."

I saw a few of the students note down the information as

if it were new. While this was the second week of the new term, this should have been covered on the first day. I can see now why they sent me to audit this course. I watched as the professor nervously opened a small tablet to control the lights and projected images for her presentation. The lights dimmed and she began her preface.

"As you know, I am Professor Anorath," she said for my benefit. "Today we are taking a look at the Founding Mothers and their actions that lead to the world of prosperity we now live in."

Anorath wore a white robe, which was standard for many scholars. It was a plain, loose fitting dressing robe. It was a part of the Uniformity's dictate to make the information the focus of teaching, rather than the teacher themselves. For those like me, who taught in a physical fashion, we wore close fitting body suits. Some, in a form of allowed protest, would wear their hair in a fashion otherwise not suitable for public consumption. At least in my opinion. Going to lengths to create a statement from your hair just seemed frivolous to me. But it was a great example of the freedoms allowed by the Uniformity.

The professor had simple brown hair pulled back from her face. It seemed perhaps she had the same opinion as mine, however, she could have skipped the frivolity knowing that she would be audited today.

"The Goddess, in Her wisdom," the professor continued, as I heard some long suffering sighs. "Saw fit to deliver a message through the United States of America to the World."

Being religious wasn't uncommon, but those that were not generally had little patience for the overbearing teachings of those who were.

"That message was in the form of the 2016 election, where for the first time in modern history, a woman was on the ballot to be elected President of said country. It was a horrendous time for the world. Women's rights were on the brink of being lost, the world was at war, Men ruled, and the

Earth was dying.

"Then the unthinkable happened - a Man, completely unqualified, won the elections."

There were disgusted groans, boos, and hisses from the students. I grinned at the response as the professor found her groove and began making it come to life. A picture of the man flashed across the screen.

Sallow skin peaked out at the edges of his eyes and neck underneath an awful fake tan, used to disguise his obvious health problems. Jowls and under eyes sagged heavily. His thinning straw yellow hair, awkwardly combed forward to hide his baldness. How anyone at the time couldn't see that he was suffering from late stage heart disease and dementia, I would never understand.

The scribbling sounds of students to their notepads broke the silence. Some would record the lecture on their wrist units, but the smart ones would also take physical notes on their thought pads. These were a great use of integrated technology that would connect the lecture to the notes and help future study sessions.

I had a similar thought pad, but it was a quarter of the size with twice the functionality as those sold to students. I saw a few eager looks in my direction as I used the holographic function to clear out some outdated messaging as I watched the lecture.

"His name is lost to history, as it was banned from being said around 2050," Anorath continued once the jeers had died down. "Our fore-mothers, in their infinite wisdom, knew that he and his offspring, were they still alive today, would be best forgotten rather than being recorded in the annals of historia.

"Why do we still call it HIS-storia then?" A student blurted out. "Isn't that still a tribute to men?"

An instant discussion broke out and I noted down how long it took for the professor to get the students under control.

"Would you like an answer or would you like to debate amongst yourselves?" She finally asked the room.

Silence followed, though there were some grumbles.

"This is a divisive tactic used by some polarizing factions," Anorath stated. "As a World law, we did change the word History to Historia. This was a conscious decision on the Uniformity's part to distance itself in part from the negative intonement created by men throughout the Annals. However, just like our legal system, the word comes from Ancient Greek and is actually genderless. And it means, learning or knowing by inquiry. That's it. Now, as I was saying..."

To catch up, Anorath moved quickly through the next sections. She spent little time on the election itself, and its major elections fraud, but moved on to year 2019 when the unthinkable continued.

"In 2019, when women thought they were safe, a series of bills were introduced in which no one thought would pass both the House and the Senate. Can anyone tell me what Roe v. Wade is?"

Every hand shot up. Rather than wait to be called on, one student answered.

"It was the 1973 landmark decision of the U.S. Supreme Court in which the Court ruled that the Due Process Clause of the Fourteenth Amendment to the U.S. Constitution provides a fundamental 'right to privacy' that protects a pregnant woman's liberty to choose whether or not to have an abortion."

All the hands dropped in disappointment.

"Exactly right, and what happened in 2019?" Anorath asked.

A few hands shot up this time, but another student answered quickly catching onto the style of teaching.

"It was overturned."

"What came next?"

"The death penalty or a stripping of voting rights, depending on the state and whether or not they allowed the death penalty."

"The same as if we were murderers," Anorath noted.

"Was it limited to only women?"

"No!" Several students shouted.

"Right," Anortha nodded. "These laws included the doctors who would perform abortions, anyone who helped someone obtain one, anyone who withheld information or failed to report. Soon there were public executions of representatives in both the House and Senate of the United States Congress for anyone who opposed the Bill, and it was legal for them to do so.

"This led to the Grand Old Party owning the entire government and passing the repeal of what Amendment next?"

"The 19th!" Someone shouted.

"And what amendment was that?"

"The right for women to vote", said a quiet voice from the front.

"Correct," Anorath beamed. "Such smart people I have here. This one is a bit harder, can anyone tell me why it was justified?"

The room was silent. No one could find a logical reason, because there wasn't one.

"Because they wanted complete and total power," I stated.

"True," Anorath. "But not exactly what I was looking for. They justified it, saying that anyone willing to kill an unborn child should be stripped of their rights."

"But that's hypocritical!" One student shouted, and others chimed in.

"Also true, but that's all the time we have for today," Anorath powered down her projector and the lights grew again. "Remember to do your reading assignments."

I stood and waved to the professor as I glided out the door while the students were packing up.

I'd heard it all before, but I wasn't a fan of their religious bent on the past. I preferred unbiased and unembellished, even dry, facts. There was still a separation of Church and Union, as it were. Any religious classes were strictly elective and counted for less credits than their official counterparts. The classes themselves were only allowed to be held after the standard schedule had ended.

I'd say that Professor Anorath did fine during her presentation, however, I would have to note that she may have forgotten to add the religious disclaimer to her first day of classes. It would have given students a chance to change classes if they felt uncomfortable with the view point. Overall, it was the same information relayed so in the end it didn't really matter as long as the students were passing the tests. I walked down the hall toward the stairs; hopped down two at a time and let the doors to the street swing wide as I exited the building.

I breathed in the cool air deeply and let its chill touch my skin. I wished for a moment that I'd brought a jacket, then began to jog. I would be home soon anyway. In this territory, September was when the weather began to turn chilly. My skin warmed quickly and my breathing was even. The steady pat of my feet hitting the ground was always a comfort to me. Physical activities have always come easy for me. It was one reason why I'd been chosen as Hoplomachos for this region's college.

As I ran, I thought back to the classroom, and our bloody history of oppression.

Men, I scoffed.

It was hard for me to believe there had been a time that women were subjugated, even reviled. The idea that a *man* had complete control of the law making process and could strip a woman of her autonomy. It just seemed ridiculous.

I ran under the banners that were being raised above the nearby street for this weekend.

The Centennial Celebration, they seemed to scream with their bright colors.

It had been almost exactly one-hundred years since the formation of the Uniformity after The Scourge had wreaked havoc in our world and rendered men completely helpless. I would say useless, but they'd already proven themselves useless by the time The Scourge hit.

Police states. Threats of Nuclear War. Unfettered access to weapons of mass destruction. Monied lobbyists running around like children buying laws like candy. Outlawing the personal production of food, so that you were completely dependent on the economy, and when that crashed, the government for support. Stealing money from the poor in order to pay debts they had no part in creating. Holes in the ozone layer and chemicals poisoning the food. No clean drinking water. Starving children in what they had termed "first world" nations, that were supposed to me the richest in wealth. Death. Destruction. Disease. Famine. The list went on and on.

In my opinion, there hadn't been much of a difference between "first" and "third" world nations in regards to the starving. Both had hungry, malnourished children sleeping and dying in the street's fetid back allies. Both had ruling classes that could do something about it, but chose not to. There had been enough wealth and food production to solve hunger and homelessness. However, the oligarchs had decided to turn a blind eye in order to conserve their third, forth, or fifth ridiculously opulent vacation home.

The opulent homes that had survived the wars were still in use, but no one was allowed to own one, let alone multiple. They were properties of the Uniformity and used for public co-op housing in many cases. I could think of just a hand full in the entire world that were retained as residences through charity working loopholes. I, unfortunately, knew one of these personally.

Within the last one-hundred years women had taken over and fixed nearly everything. Almost every disease had been eradicated. No child was left without food or education. There was still death of course, but we hadn't found the natural end of a lifespan yet. There were still women alive who had been born during the Age of Men.

The record so far was one-hundred-forty.

There were still some pockets of violence, acts that were still perpetrated by men. The main offender was a small resistance group calling themselves Vengeance. However, they weren't taken very seriously. Not many men had made it through The Scourge unharmed.

Another mark of their stupidity.

A man had thought it would be a good idea to use Nuclear Power as a "clean and renewable" source of energy.

I laughed outright as I ran. Headlines came back to me from that time that I'd researched for my dissertation stating that it was the safest resource. Well, that had turned and bit them, hadn't it? The Scourge had eventually been tracked to the source, a nuclear spill that had gone unnoticed and seeped into the drinking water. It had bred in the area that was known as the United States, and began to spread. This country had been one of the worst contributors to the men's oppression of women since its inception, some 400 years ago.

The Scourge, a terrible nerve disease, had spread like wildfire. It attached to the Y chromosome and severely inhibited the production of testosterone. Men got sick, flabby, and weak. Instances of rape dropped to nothing, and suddenly the women of that time looked around and realized they were all that was left. Since then all power plants of that nature had been dismantled and quarantined, but the damage had already been done.

The real tragedy had been in the male babies that were created during that time with men who had a broken Y chromosome. They were born severely sick and didn't live long, though many of them never even made it to term. The girls produced were healthy and without physical impairments. There were a few places that had remained untouched by The Scourge, though not many. The Amish and the Quakers were a few of the small introverted societies spared. Their lack of communication and outreach into their surrounding countries, historians gather, is most likely what saved them from The Scourge.

They were given amnesty and independence from the new World Government. They were allowed to continue governing themselves, provided that they supplied healthy sperm from their men upon request from the government, in case we needed to diversify the gene pool. There were only five colonies in the entire world that were allowed to live that way. Everywhere else had become a utopian matriarchy. One free of want and war. These colonies didn't mind that the world had changed completely around them, they had disapproved of the world before and continued to disapprove today. They had a right to their opinion, even if it was wrong.

Every person had a purpose, and that purpose aligned with their wants and needs. Because of this, the level of life satisfaction remained high.

Of course some were still unhappy but as yet there was no cure for that, though there were treatment options if one sought it.

I jogged past the row houses. Not much had changed in these buildings or streets. They were well kept and maintained. The infrastructure within the Uniformity was Primary, as it directly affected everyone. Leafy trees lined both sides of the street. Not many cars were on the roads at the moment, but there were cyclists and joggers aplenty.

Obesity was another product of a bygone age that had, for the most part, been eradicated. If someone was overweight now, it was a direct result of their choices. Thyroid issues and genetic problems were not viable diseases anymore. Seeing pictures of people from the early 21st century was mind boggling. The rampant overeating and lack of access to real nutrients was astonishing. It was amazing that you could find food anywhere, but none of it was really life sustaining. It's not surprising that the average life expectancy was only 65.

Now there was an easy solution to get what your body needed. A specific ration diet and supplements were prescribed during your yearly health exam. The ration flavors were specifically designed to appeal to your palate, and they kept your stomach satisfied. Luxury food items, like deserts and unhealthy foods, still existed, but they were in low demand. Everything you needed was provided for you at a minimal cost. Capitalism still existed, but only with non-essential products like jewelry and fashion clothing.

It had been outlawed to capitalize on the pain of the less fortunate, or provide them a lesser service. All necessities were tightly regulated and controlled so that everyone paid the same, regardless of their standing in society. This included housing, basic clothing, food rations, water, utilities, power, internet access, and anything else the body needed to be healthy and complete.

Within one-hundred years, after the failures of men for thousands of years, women were able to create a paradise on Earth.

However, not everyone was happy with their standing in life.

I paused to stretch at an intersection and watched a small gathering of four masked figures that were quietly holding signs.

Their signs read:

See Me

Include Me

Name Me

SIN is what you live when you take a voice

I heard the sound of drones and sirens at the same time the four masked men did. They scattered. I thought about helping catch them, but I wasn't in the mood for a chase. I wanted to be home with a nice warm drink.

I finished stretching and continued down the street as I wondered why they ran. It wasn't illegal to protest. More than likely didn't have a permit to assemble. It was rare for a man to be granted a permit, and even then it was usually granted to his handler, if they were feeling generous. The rights of men had been stripped, as they had been judged incapable of the responsibility. They weren't slaves exactly, but it was close. Slavery of men had been made illegal in 2100. A turn of the century promise kept by the Uniformity.

My stomach turned, as it always did when I thought about this aspect of our Utopia.

This was the only thing I truly disagreed with, but I didn't see an acceptable alternative to maintain the paradise that women had created. My mother always told me that the world was like a swinging pendulum, and maybe men would get the chance to prove themselves worthy of these rights. But now it was still too soon to consider it.

Knowing this didn't mean that I felt good whenever I walked by those that were just trying to make the most of a situation designed to humiliate them.

Just a block from my home I passed a boutique designed for men's clothing. Though clothing was a loose term, as most of the outfits barely covered anything at all. They were all designed to show off the man's physique for a woman's ogling pleasure. One of the living mannequins in the window sported a jaunty baker's hat, a short apron that provided no real protection from a hot oven or stove, and heeled boots not unlike the combat ones I was currently wearing. His eyes looked bored, until they made eye contact with mine. A quick shine and wink made me think he'd been trained well.

I slowed to a trot as the tiny pedestal he stood on turned to reveal the back side of the outfit. Beneath the apron he wore nothing but a lacy thong, showing off the firm glute implants and a bulging pouch hidden by the tiny apron. Whether it was from stuffing or his own natural endowments I wasn't sure, and I didn't particularly want to stop and study.

The man's body had been perfectly sculpted into the perfect image of male beauty that many required from their houseboys, or the men they employed.

I walked the last block to my own little brownstone row house. It was a quick jog from the recruitment offices where I worked out of when I wasn't training. At the moment my job was overseeing first combat experiences for our new recruits.

Walking up the steps, I took out a key from the interior pocket of my skin shorts. They hugged my hips and ended at my knee, in standard-issue black of course. I pulled the long black tank top I wore back down over my hips. It had ridden up during my run to just under my utility belt, which was wrapped around my waist and secured by outside straps to both of my thighs. I began to position the key to unlock the door but froze as I reached it.

My door stood slightly ajar. The interior was dark.

I replaced my key, activated my wrist unit to record my actions and slowly moved my hands to the weapon I carried in my thigh holster.

Before I let any doubts cloud my judgement I moved forward into the darkness, swiftly and absolutely silent, my weapon drawn. I ignored the stairs straight ahead, and instead went in low and to the right. I passed through the dining room and around the small corner to the left. There was a small nook, I remember thinking would come in handy in just such an occasion. Vaguely I acknowledged that my heart was pounding, though it had been steady just moments before, after the run. I held my back to the wall next to the window as I crouched even lower to probe the darkness of my home with my eyes and ears.

A small rustle came from the living room to the left of the entrance.

Instead of moving straight to the target I kept my back to the wall and moved around the perimeter of my tiny kitchen, into the small hallway under the stairs that wrapped the first floor toward the living room. I checked the back door, which was still locked and unbroken. Then I moved, quiet as a shadow, into my living room. It ran the entire length of the first floor, flanked on either end by an exterior door.

A figure ahead of me stood casually facing the doorway I'd entered through.

I moved up directly behind them ready to attack, then I

stopped dead as I caught scent of a deeply floral perfume. I straightened as I recognized it.

"Mom?" I whispered.

She let out a startled yelp and the lights flashed on, blinding me for a moment as a few people yelled, "Surprise!"

"My goodness, Casandra!" My mother blathered over the shouts. "You scared me half to death."

I scared you? I thought, as I holstered my weapon and my heart began to calm.

"Sorry, mom," I forced a smile and gave her the hug I knew that she was expecting.

"What's the occasion?" I asked when we broke apart, seeing my free weekend slip slowly down the drain.

"You are, of course!" She exclaimed. "Did you forget your birthday again? You are hopeless."

She tsked as she steered me to a seat.

I smiled at the small gathering, as one by one they offered me a happy birthday. I'd known them all casually for years, as friends of my mother. Except for one new addition. She had a shock of red hair, pulled straight up at the sides then exploding in curls from the top, like a mushroom cloud. She was long and gangly, seeming to be around eighteen. Her eyes were a deep blue, like the sea at night, and she looked everywhere except at me. She wore a modern version of mid-twentieth century punk attire, which was the fashion trend currently making the rounds as a form of protest to the current etiquette of dress. Ripped black fishnets, frayed black shorts, a bright red corset, and a black leather jacket covered her body. The same heeled combat boots I'd seen on the shop boy in the window display earlier graced her feet. Dark eye liner, and lipstick to match her corset and hair. Her body language said that she really did not want to be there.

I let my eyes wander back to the women surrounding her. They all wore similar outfits, varying only in size and color. Pencil skirts, heels, a plain shirt that matched the color of her shoes, finished with a blazer that matched the skirt.

Five women in the group overall, excluding myself and my mother.

My birthday wasn't until next week, but since today would consist of a parade through the main streets of town, I could see why my mother had planned something for now. I hid the sigh I felt. I should have anticipated this party.

Mother was always one for combining celebrations whenever possible.

A man walked through the room, dressed conservatively

in a white button down shirt and black slacks. He carried a platter of fluted glasses containing a bubbling liquid the color of sunsets in one hand, and balanced another tray full of some dainty puffed pastries with his other. The women talked amongst themselves as I took a flute and smiled at their inane chatter. Bobbing my head anytime a question winged its way toward me.

There was a reason I didn't have friends.

"Now, you have a drink and gab for a bit, then I want you to run upstairs and get dressed," my mother commanded. "I'm going to finish making the arrangements for this weekend."

I bit my lip to stop myself from grabbing her, shaking her. Instead I took a deep breath and smiled at the group again. As she walked away talking at her wrist unit, absently making lists, I noticed the teenager studying me. As soon as I turned my head, she whipped her gaze away.

"How old are you now dear?" One of my mother's friends, Eugenia, asked, pulling my attention from the girl.

She was wearing a lavender and baby pink version of their high society uniforms. My mother and her friends were directly responsible for Charity Events, the company that my mother had founded to direct funds to lesser known issues that may have fallen through the cracks in our local society. It held her namesake, Charity Casey, and as such it seemed like it was meant to be.

"Twenty-five next week," I stated, then took a sip of my drink.

It tasted of berries and a light fizz I identified as a sparkling white wine. A favorite of my mother's, as the grapes are grown in her personal vineyard.

"Such a wonderful time to be alive!" Another of my mother's friends, Josephine, stated and they all nodded, giggling. Josephine was wearing a dark navy and turquoise combination. "My granddaughter Skyye just turned eighteen! I can hardly believe it. Feels like just yesterday I was eighteen and going to my deflowering."

And there it was.

I watched the teenager squirm from the corner of my eye.

Mother sure did like to combine events. So it was to be a DeFlowering tonight? Fine.

"Skyye is it?" I turned towards the girl casually. She cringed slightly before making eye contact with me.

"Would you like to freshen up while I'm changing?" I asked.

"Oh what a great idea!" Josephine crowed. "Yes, you two go upstairs."

I smiled and nodded toward the stairs. I didn't wait to see if she would follow. If she was smart then she would be, though the fact that she had agreed to an antiquated ritual like a deflowering made that idea dubious. But I understood familial pressure.

If I didn't, then I could have easily snuck out the back door as soon as I realized what was happening in my living room.

I pulled my shirt off as I entered my room and began unbuckling the fasteners on my utility belt. I walked to the closet and entered my keycode, as well as my fingerprint, into the wall safe located next to the sliding pocket doors. I never bothered to hide the location behind a painting, as the safe had been designed for. Theft was irregular, and everyone in the surrounding area knew who I was. They likely thought there would be booby traps.

I chuckled as I stowed my weapon, harness, and utility belt.

"What's so funny?" Skyye's voice came from the doorway.

"I was just thinking about other people's opinions of me," I turned, naked from the waist up, and gestured to a lounging chair next to the door. "Close the door behind you."
I turned my back to her and heard the click of the door.

"The room is soundproof," I stated. "So you're welcome

to vent your frustration or excitement."

I unlaced my boots and toed them off, then pulled down my pants so that I stood in nothing but a standard issue black thong. I walked into my closet and stared at my clothes.

"Or," I called when she didn't immediately begin. "You can ask questions from someone who has experienced a deflowering first hand."

"You?!" Skyye squeaked.

"Yes," I looked over my shoulder. "Me."

"But you're not religious," Skyye said, more as a question than a statement, looking around my room for any sign of the Goddess.

"Not now," I returned and began rifling through my dress section.

Remembering how it was chilly outside, I chose a long sweater dress in my favorite color, hunter green, and black leggings. After quickly throwing them on I stepped back into my combat boots. I had more shoes, but I was compromising with the dress. I walked to the long wall of mirrors that stood as the backsplash behind a double vanity. Everything was where I'd left it on the counters, and clean. I surveyed the image I saw in the mirror above and decided to pull my hair down.

I took it from the tail I'd placed it in when I went to work and watched the curls spring forth. I frowned at the mess and grabbed a brush to try to do some damage control.

"No questions?" I prodded.

"Well," Skyye's voice drifted off as she watched me wet and tame the curls so they behaved, ending just above my shoulders. "I was wondering what it's like..."

"It's however you want it to be like," I smiled at her reflection in the mirror. "It's your choice, no one else's. No one else is going to be in the room with you."

I remembered the nerves I felt when I was in her place so long ago.

"What's your fantasy?" I asked and began applying a light

amount of makeup.

"A beautiful woman," Skyye said, a bit too quickly.

"Are you sure?" I paused and studied her.

Her eyes filled and her lips quivered.

"Hey," I set down my lipstick.

Now I understood the real reason my mother had combined celebrations.

"Look," I handed her a tissue from the nightstand and crouched in front of her. "This is about you and your choice. Have you had sex before?"

Skyye shook her head and blew her nose.

"Ok," I smiled. "See you're one step better than me."

Skyye let out a watery laugh.

"Do you want to have sex?"

Skyye nodded shyly.

"Do you want to have sex with a woman?" I asked point blank.

Skyye held her breath and I saw the answer in her eyes.

"No," she whispered.

I patted her leg encouragingly.

"That's ok," I smiled. "That's the best part about the deflowering ceremony. No one will know but you and the person you choose."

"Really?" She asked me, hopefully.

"Really," I nodded once then stood to finish my makeup.

"My first time with a man was during my deflowering ceremony," I told her.

"It was?" Skyye gasped.

"Yep," I laughed at her expression of shock. "You get to pick whatever scene with whatever person you choose. No one gets to see the itinerary unless you show them, and you can do what you want."

"Were you nervous?" She asked me.

"A little," I nodded. "But I wanted to see what the fuss was about. These ceremonies are old school. Something invented by our foremothers at the turn of the century, to keep a semblance of religion and morals within their grasp. But they also came from a time of puritanism. This seemed like such a liberating idea back then. Taking control of your virginity."

"Now it just seems..." Skyye trailed off.

"Suffocating?" I asked and she nodded. "You know you can say no and wait until you're ready."

"I'm ready," she said quickly, then paused. "I'm just nervous about my mother finding out that I had sex with a man."

"Ah," I sighed as I finished my makeup. "She's a purist?"

I watched Skyye nod sadly.

"Well," I shrugged. "Just don't tell her."

"But what if..."

"She won't find out," I said firmly as I surveyed the finished results of my handiwork in the mirror.

My soft brown hair curled above my shoulders, cheekbones that demanded attention rose high on my cheeks. I'd lined my eyes with a soft gold to accent the sweater dress I wore. My nose was a bit broad for my taste, but spoke, like my cheekbones, to my First Nations heritage. The eyes I'd lined looked more brown than green currently, but that changed easily with my mood as well as my clothing choices. I wore no jewelry. I nodded at my reflection and turned back to Skyye, taking her hands and pulling her up.

"She will not find out," I repeated as I strapped my weapon back on my thigh. "Unless you tell her. But..."

I waited until she made eye contact with me. Those tumultuous sea-at-night eyes flashed.

"You need to remember that you can never have a real relationship with a man," I said the words slowly, making sure they sunk in. "They will always try to put themselves above you. They are haunting and attractive, but they cannot be trusted. Not now. Not ever."

I watched as her eyes hardened and she nodded.

"This isn't just fairytales of the boogeyman," I reminded

her. "Use men for what you need, but you cannot give up your power to them or let them make you think they can be relied on. They will always let you down."

"It sounds like you're speaking from experience," Skyye pulled her hands from mine.

I frowned as my head began to hurt.

"No," I stated. "I'm just well versed in Historia. Don't let it happen to you."

Skyye nodded again and I smiled, moving to the door. I opened it and gestured.

"Shall we?"

When she moved out ahead of me, a feeling of deja vu nearly overwhelmed me. I shook it away and closed the door to my bedroom before following her down the stairs.

The streets were filled with people downtown. Fridays were usually a busy time for the area, as many of the Uniformity came here to cut loose.

Loud and boisterous music pounded from inside the clubs that lined the streets around us. Laughter and shouts surrounded our small group as we moved through the crowd. Our destination was at the end of the block - the only quiet tea room and sex club in the city.

Most clubs were loud, rowdy and, in these ladies opinions, undignified.

Deflowering was an antiquated ritual, born of Religious Zealotry, and forced impregnation. Those that held to the old beliefs tended to be a bit more well off financially and very old-world. "Set in their ways" would be a more accurate description. The practice began some time in the early 21st century, not long after The Scourge hit. The rise of a fascist nation run by women with a concrete foundation of beliefs called The Way of the Goddess.

The idea behind Deflowering had been to take back the practice of forced marriage and public deflowering, and made it a rite of passage within the control of women. Or, more accurately, the woman's mother or guardian.

I scanned the crowd actively, even though I knew there would be no threats here. The Resistance would be stupid to attack the heart of the Uniformity during the Centennial Celebration. But that didn't affect my conditioning to always be on guard. It was ingrained, as it should have been in those women who laughed and shouted around me.

I pushed away the feeling of envy of their ability to compartmentalize so easily. I'd learned long ago that I was different. It was why I didn't hold onto friends - I was never able to cut loose. It got old for them very quickly that my demeanor was not a front.

I could drink most people under the table and they would never know the extent of my inebriation. To most people I was a "stick-in-the-mud" because I didn't enjoy letting my guard down. I wasn't really sure why, but I never felt safe. It's why I didn't have a dog or other sort of pet animal. If there was a strange noise in my house, I needed to know that it wasn't supposed to be there.

My senses were always attuned to the slightest noise, even while sleeping. I made sure my row house was soundproofed, even though noise pollution was a thing of the past. I was an incredibly light sleeper, anything would wake me from a sound sleep. Many couldn't stand the silence. I reveled in it.

When a pedestrian I was passing bumped my shoulder, I instinctively turned to see their face. Though his baggy hood was up and he was hunched I could tell he was more than six-feet tall, which was rare. His choice of clothing was what drew my attention, because he obviously didn't want to be seen. Even with bone extensions and implants it was rare for men to exceed five feet, since their growth hormones had been affected by The Scourge.

I looked down to see if maybe his height was due to boots, but he wore flat sneakers. He turned his head just enough so I could see sharp blue eyes. When they connected with mine they seemed to widen, in surprise or recognition I couldn't tell, before he abruptly turned and was lost in the crowd.

That same sense of deja vu kicked me in the gut and I knew something was wrong. With so many people around I couldn't very well yell fire, but I needed to do something.

I tapped Skyye on the shoulder and whispered in her ear.

"I'll catch up," I told her. "I just need to make a quick phone call."

"Please don't leave," Skyye turned and grabbed my hand. Her look of panic returned.

"I will be there in time," I smiled reassuringly. "Don't worry."

Skyye frowned, but reluctantly let go of my hand.

I melted into the crowd and found a relatively quiet spot in an alley nearby. Touching my wrist unit, I entered a code used for securing encrypted messages.

"What is it?" Came a gruff and harried voice, yawning.

"There might be a problem," I answered and spoke about what I'd seen.

"There is no basis for evacuating the area," the voice sighed. "But continue to monitor the area and we will alert active agents nearby."

"Good," I rubbed the base of my neck where an ache had begun to form.

"You know there has been zero Resistance activity in your area," the voice reminded me.

"I know, but something seemed off," I replied. "I would rather have reported and be prepared, than not report and risk lives."

"Your duty has been done," said the voice, sounding annoyed that I'd chastised them.

"Exousia," I stated the formal sign off.

"Exousia," they repeated and I ended the communication.

I breathed deep and began walking back the way I'd come. The Uniformity knew I was good at my job, but sometimes I wondered if they thought I was overly cautious. There had been zero attacks from the Resistance for almost five years. The Uniformity was always watching, and there had even been talk lately that the Resistance had fallen. I did not agree.

I stepped back out onto the busy street and saw that not much had changed. Then, as if they'd heard my thoughts, the wrist units of every Uniformity soldier in the area chimed. Everyone looked at their units and there was a deafening quiet; then, as if nothing had changed, the cacophony of sound began again.

Everyone in the area had been warned that there may be a threat. I saw a few on-duty officers flanking parts of the street stand a little straighter, look around a little sharper. That was all I could expect with the information I'd given them.

I did my best to put it all aside. I hurried my pace to catch up with my party, which had been detained just outside the target building. They were speaking to a group of women around the same age, toting another eighteen-year-old. This one, however, seemed much more enthused to be there as she gushed her excitement at a very unenthusiastic Skyye.

Her blonde hair bounced, traditional white dress, complete with ruffles and a hoop skirt. I would have felt bad for the girl, if she didn't look so pleased with herself. She'd probably picked out the dress herself.

Women still married now, but it was more of a female partnership than anything else. Marrying men was possible but it was frowned upon harshly by most in society. Financially, there was no benefit to marrying a man. They couldn't hold property, own a business, and most couldn't even provide healthy sperm for propagation. However, it still happened.

More often women, if they were so inclined, made an advantageous match with a financially upward momentum and kept a male as a toy to be played with and exchanged, or kept for as long as they wanted.

So the traditional white dress of the ancient misogynistic Christian belief system had been moved to a woman's deflowering, as they were no longer expected to be virginal when they wed. The idea of dawning white and then disposing of it by your own choice was purely symbolic now.

The girl in white nearly vibrated as her hair continued to bounce.

The building in front of them rose ominously above. Its style was reminiscent of a bygone Victorian age when women, of a certain class, were only expected to sit prettily, drink tea, make babies, and occasionally sew. It had a small outdoor courtyard surrounded by a black wrought iron fence. The pointed tips of the rods rose well above six feet.

Inside the fence there was a recreation of an old Victorian home complete with: high-rising turrets, peaked roofs, and gargoyles keeping watch. It was like a tiny castle.

The first stage in a deflowering ceremony,was tea in a formal dining room for the initiate and their guests as she perused her choices. Beautiful women and men were paraded around naked for her enjoyment, adorned only with numbers painted on their backs.

The women that participated in these rituals were well known, as they usually taught sexual pleasure classes as well as basic biology courses. Both were required to graduate from primary school, typically at thirteen, before you chose a Bent.

A Bent being: a path in which you would eventually select your career. If you were interested in the sexual aspects of life and enjoyed having sex, you were always able to join a House of Perpetual Pleasure, or HoPP for short.

There were many forms of these houses, and they weren't just for deflowering ceremonies. The sexual shame of the Puritans had been shed long ago. There was a short resurgence during the wars, but without men to use shame and sex to control women it died out quickly.

My mother, who was talking to the female barring the gate to the House, was gesturing angrily as I finished my approach.

"What do you mean, you're closed?" My mother demanded. "I called just an hour ago to confirm our reservation."

"I know, and I'm so sorry Ms. Casey," the woman apologized. "We had an unexpected issue come up."

"What kind of issue would close this house?" My mother ground out through clenched teeth.

"I'm not at liberty to divulge that information right now," the woman was nearly in tears as the crowd around her grew. She slipped behind the gate, attaching a sign as she did. "I'm really, really sorry."

The woman turned and ran into the darkened House. I studied the sign.

Closed Until Further Notice

"Well," my mother huffed and turned back to our small

party. "I guess we will need to find another House for the ceremony."

The crowd that had gathered to watch the exchange dispersed.

"But I wanna go here!" The girl in the white dress stomped her foot, suddenly looking much younger than the 18 she supposedly was.

"I know baby," a woman I would assume was her mother crooned.

She was dressed in an off white pant suit, not unlike the uniform of the women I was with.

"Someone probably rented the entire HOPP for themselves," someone in the crowd murmured as they began walking away.

"Where else is there?" Skyye asked softly, a small note of hope peeking through.

"That would be up to you, dear," Josephine, her grandmother, prodded.

"If I can't go here, then I'm not deflowering today!" The girl in white screeched.

I twitched. That level of self absorption always set my nerves on edge.

"That's fine, baby," the woman took her by the hand and led her away. "Whatever you want."

I stared after them as they made their way through the crowded streets. The girl nearly kicked and screamed as they went.

I did not envy the girl and her eventual arrival into reality. She would have a shock when she went into the workforce. My mother had babied my younger sister the same way, and that had ended very badly.

Though some, I thought of Victoria, *never truly give up on self-absorption.*

I pushed away the memories that threatened to invade. No need for guilt. Not tonight. I did what was right.

I turned back to Skyye and the rest of the group. Skyye

looked at me with a small helpless gaze.

"I think I know a place," I said to the group. "It's not far. Just a little off the beaten path. I think Skyye will love it."

Skyye relaxed visibly and nodded.

"Great!" I tried to effuse enthusiasm. "This way."

I turned and took a meandering pace toward our new destination.

Leaving the crowded streets behind, I could hear the clip of the ladies' sensible heels behind me more easily. The clap of the heeled boots Skyye wore was also now audible. I didn't need to glance behind me to know that they were all there. They chatted about birthdays and functions as we walked. I turned down a dark alley and felt the tone change.

"Now just a moment!" One of the ladies called from behind me.

"Oh hush," my mother scolded. "Casandra knows where we are going. I trust her implicitly."

Her statement cramped my stomach. I pushed the feeling of misplaced guilt away again. I reminded myself that it hadn't been my fault. When a woman came of age, some just weren't prepared for their responsibilities to our Society.

I pushed forward a bit further then stopped suddenly, holding out a hand motioning the party to stop.

I turned directly to the left and knocked, three sharp taps and one pound with my fist. An old iron peephole slid rustily to the left, revealing a set of steady, golden eyes.

"Ah, Dekka Casey," the woman on the other side chortled. "Back again are we? I didn't think we'd see you this soon."

"Plans changed," I smiled. "I brought some friends."

"Friends?" The eyes moved over my shoulder to the women behind me. "Indeed. Well, formalities must be observed. Password?"

"Pertinacious," I told her and watched as the eyes crinkled.

"That is indeed your word," the peephole slid shut again,

then I could hear the heavy locks being disengaged.

"Is this..." Skyye whispered reverently behind me.

The thick wooden door opened to reveal the owner of the golden eyes, though you actually needed to look much farther down than the peephole to see her. She wore a frilled white and pink dress, like an old porcelain doll. Her face was just as starkly white, with lips, eyes and cheeks painted the same garish pink. Her almond-shaped eyes glowed in the dim lighting that filtered in from the alley. Behind her was darkness.

"Welcome," she bowed deeply and swept the way with her left hand, holding the door open with her right. "To GrandIloquence."

I stepped aside so the others could proceed before me. I saw Skyye's face split into an excited grin as she disappeared into the dark entry.

"Thanks Violet," I told the doorwoman. I passed her as the last of my party to enter, and heard the metal clank of the bolts locking behind me.

A small candle was flickering in the nook behind the door, lighting her face in an eerie glow.

"Anything for one of our best customers," she winked at me and crawled back up onto the tall stool. When sitting she was at eye level with me once again. "Why the change of plans? I thought you were looking forward to a quiet weekend alone."

"My mom was helping someone throw a deflowering," I sighed. "And decided to throw me a birthday party so that I would come along."

"Mothers," Violet exaggeratingly shook her head sadly. "So out of touch."

I half smiled and turned to follow the party, which had moved towards the sound of revelry deeper in the establishment. I walked forward a few feet then took the stairs downward.

This place had become a favorite of mine recently because

of the clientele. I enjoyed indulging my passion for people watching here. With only two exits, the main entrance and an emergency tunnel below the bar, I was able to relax as much as I possibly could. That, and the fact that this bar was a well kept secret, meant that there wasn't ever a crush of people. It had been built in an old storage basement, originally used as an illegal still operation during the first round of prohibition in the early twentieth century. That was why there were the tunnels, for the distribution of prohibited intoxicants. Unfortunately, when The Scourge hit, the idea of reinstating prohibition seemed like the right choice for the transitional time. Of course, the speakeasy was once again used for its intended purpose. After prohibition failed for a second time it was named GrandIloquence, and opened to members only, which helped keep it private and low-key. A member could bring friends, but each password is unique to its patrons.

I continued down the stairs and through the hallway, which ended at the candlelit main chamber that was GrandIloquence. When I saw the look of star struck pleasure on Skyye's face I forgave my mother for this inconvenience. If I could make this girl's entrance into womanhood easier in any way, then I would sleep easy tonight.

I grabbed the nearest server and let them know we were here for a DeFlowering Ceremony, knowing they would take care of the rest.

Considering the fact that GrandIloquence was underground, it was surprisingly well lit. They had limited power, for ambiance rather than need. The power problems of the world had been solved near the beginning of the formation of the Uniformity. Once the ego of men and greed corporations had been taken out of the scarcity mindset, so many of the world's problems had been solved nearly overnight.

There were fluorescent lights installed but they were almost never used during business hours. The ceiling was covered in mirrors that domed around lit candles, reflecting their light to the floor and tables. The ceiling rose about four and a half meters high, and the mirrors made it seem even higher.

A few extra mirrors were used to spotlight pieces of art on the walls, the bar, and of course the small thrust stage. The art was mainly women, in all their nude glory in various professional positions. An officer for the Uniformity with her badge pinned through skin to her bare chest. A surrogate with her stomach and breasts swollen from the child she carried. A contortionist in an absurd position with her back to ten saluting leaders who faced away toward a multitude of naked women saluting back at them, the rank of Staratego tattooed on their naked backs. What drew the most attention and debate from this painting was the penis that stemmed from between her legs where her labia majora would normally be. Every face visible on every piece of artwork was either shrouded or blurred, except this one. This one had a mirror shaped to move with the painting so that when you stood in front of it, yours was the face within the contortionist.

This was one of the more hotly debated art pieces in this space to say the least, and the walls were covered in canvasses that ranged from realism to absurdism. I stood for a moment in front of the contortionist and imagined, as I always did, the pain of dysphoria for those who were born in bodies that never quite felt like their own.

Transitioning was still a hotly debated topic, even today. There were Binary Purists and there were those who fought for Trans rights. It was rare to find anyone who did not have an opinion on the subject. I could tell who was which by their reactions to this painting, which is one reason why I absolutely loved it. As I turned away and toward the stage, I could see in the reactions of those I'd brought here, who was a Purist and who was not in the looks of disdain or amusement I received. I could tell that even within my mother's group, the opinions were split. I could tell she was exasperated, but I only really had eyes for Skyye. Her eyes were wide as she took in everything as quickly as could, dripping with excitement. This was a much more welcome expression than the downcast acquiescence I'd encountered earlier.

I chose this bar specifically for its Trans employees and diverse sex workers, as well as its outstanding entertainment.

A black curtain that was drawn over the apron of the stage covered its inner workings of traps and pulleys that worked under it. It ended abruptly in front of three equidistance standing tables. Or nearly equidistance. I noted that the middle table was just off the center mark.

From the floor to the walls, the decor was dark cherrywood. The floors were marked with deep scratches and general wear from the clients, so it was a few shades lighter than the walls.

Long tables, descending in height as the space moved toward the stage, were nearly filled. A performance was underway - a vaudevillian actress juggled lit torches while balancing on a unicycle. Someone accompanied her on the piano to a jaunty tune behind the red curtain that ran the length of the background. The woman wore white face makeup to look like a crying mime. Her black and white striped jumpsuit was embellished with a pink tutu, currently the only color on the stage apart from the red fire curtain.

Oohs and *Ahhs* from the crowd displayed their pleasure at the entertainment. Three small black dogs, all wearing pink tutus to match their fellow entertainer, jumped up on their hind legs and started hopping around her unicycle as she balanced. Quiet conversations could be heard as we walked farther into the room to find a seat.

The four rows of tables sat in the middle of the room, with about three meters between the stage and the last table. There were smaller tables lining the walls that could accommodate a small group like ours. We headed for the one closest to the stage. I watched as Skyye attempted to drink in everything.

"I'll go to the bar and let them know we are here, and why," I told the group quietly as they sat. "I'm sure they'll have a party room available if we want one."

"Can we stay out here?" Skyye asked me, her eyes darting around the group.

"Whatever you would like, my dear," Josephine patted her on the shoulder.

"Alright," I smiled softly. "I'll be back with some menus."

I let the smile fade as I walked away and rubbed at my jaw. This was the most I'd smiled in months and my face was starting to hurt. But I knew what was expected of me as I slowly transitioned into the hostess of this soirée. Plus, I now felt a vested interest in Skyye's Deflowering. If a young woman didn't have someone on their side pushing for what they wanted then the whole thing could become a very uncomfortable experience. Not unlike getting a tattoo. You needed to make sure it was something you would be happy with for the rest of your life, and be able to speak up to the tattoo artist if something wasn't right. You couldn't be afraid to offend the people around you in order to make yourself truly happy.

I should know. I ran a hand unconsciously over the faded lettering on my shoulder.

Jen.

It had appeared one morning after a weekend blackout. Not one of my prouder moments. Made even worse for the realization that I had no idea who *Jen* was.

"Ah," a tall thin male stood behind the shiny bar as I approached. "Mistress Dekka, how may I assist you?"

The way he rocked back and forth on his feet told me he wore stilts under his abnormally long black dress slacks. Otherwise his nearly two meter tall frame would seem unusual. He wore a white button down shirt, with the sleeves rolled up to his elbows. A black two button vest held a gold chain that ran from the loop to his pocket, most likely holding a timepiece. In the small breast pocket of the vest was a red silk kerchief that matched his red silk bow tie.

His face was on the gaunt side. He'd more than likely been on the stilts for hours. He wore a monocle, also attached by a gold chain to the small loop at his side. His dark hair was parted in the middle and he sported a mustache that twirled up at the ends. The man's eye glowed behind the monocle, a honeyed yellow, and looked a lot larger as it was magnified by the glass.

"Amadeus!" I greeted him. "I just need some menus for my table, and one deflowering menu."

"A deflowering!" He set aside the pint glass he'd been shining on the shelf, face down. "How exciting. Let me grab those."

Amadeus handed me the menus that were right next to him and then turned to the back of the bar.

"We haven't done a deflowering in ages," he said as he reached above the cabinets that housed the various liquor selections. The back of his vest sported a beautifully stitched gear. "Female, I assume?"

"You know," I pretended to ponder. "I'm not sure, can I have both menus for now?"

"Of course!" Amadeus glowed. "You know all walks are welcome here."

"I do," I curved my lips and my cheeks twitched in pain.

Along with the menus, he pulled down the large leather bound volumes.

"We have some of the menu items on site, and others are on call," Amadeus said as he handed me the heavy menus.

"Beautiful," I said as I hefted them. "I'll bring them back shortly with the orders."

"No need," Amadeus waved me off. "I'll have Charlene take your orders."

"Ok," I pursed my lips as his unnatural height reminded me of something. "You haven't seen anyone new come through here today have you? Maybe a man untouched by scourge?"

"No," Amadeus picked up another glass to continue polishing, but something about his answer felt off. He'd answered too quickly. "I didn't think they ventured out of their little countries."

"Not often," I frowned at him as he looked away from my gaze and toward the stage. "Well, I'll get back to my people."

I nodded my thanks and turned back to join my party with the menus. I'd have to follow up with Amadeus later.

"Alright ladies," I handed out the drink and food menus, then handed the heavy leather bound menus to Skyye. "I figured it would be fun to see what's in the male menu, even if you don't want one."

I allowed myself to laugh bawdily, and wink to elicit giggles from the older women. Skyye sent me a thankful smile and opened the male and female menus together, as if comparing.

I took the seat opposite Skyye, as it was the only one left available, but it made my skin itch to sit with my back to the door. The women probably thought they were doing me a favor by saving me the seat facing closest to the stage. I had to fight my instincts and force my smile to stay in place.

Every page of the book had a picture of a male, or female, with a full description of their interests as well as weight, height, and cock/boob size. Any establishment who offered services as these had a different kind of rating system for size. It seemed garish to use inches, or the accepted metric system of measurement. So here at GrandIloquence, they used a gear system.

Each picture had a rating from one gear to 5 gears. Most of the pictures ranked between two and three gears.

"Do you think any of them chose this?" Eugenia sniffed and I held back a sigh.

Of course, if one didn't know her, one might assume she was talking about the line of work and how hard it might be. But no. She was making a comment about choosing to transition. Thankfully, I didn't need to answer.

"Eugenia, dear," my mother laughed coldly. "We aren't our parents. If a woman chooses to change her sex, then that of course would be welcomed by the community and not questioned. Right? Who are we to judge people for the choices they make in order to live their truth?"

"It's an accepted scientific fact that our gender is not binary," another of the ladies agreed with my mother.

"Oh, of course," Eugenia smiled apologetically, though I caught the looks between the other Binary Purists. "Though we can all agree that females are of course superior. That's been proven by the Utopia the Uniformity has created."

"Rejoice!" The purists responded to that statement.

"I think that we can all agree that tonight is about Skyye," I nodded toward the girl who currently had her nose nearly pressed into the menus before her. "And that her choice, just as any choice made by a woman, is hers to make."

I received some stiff nods on both sides as conversation turned to the drink menu.

Choices of that magnitude were still questioned behind closed doors. However, as a civilized society, a person's right to transition was deeply frowned upon to be spoken about negatively in public. My mother was reminding her friend, who may have had one too many drinks before we left my townhome, of this unspoken rule of etiquette. Most people who chose to transition seemed much happier and fulfilled after they did. Who were we to force a sense of rigidity in regards to what another woman needed to be happy. Even if those women were born male, they were still women.

There was a reason rates of depression and suicide among women had dropped drastically to nearly non-existent after the Binary Ban was lifted. Transitions from men to women were less often, and much more closely scrutinized, but they still happened. It just meant that if transitioning was what you truly needed and wanted, you needed to fight for it. Unfortunately, it did not change your standing in society to transition to female. As newly made women they were still not allowed to vote, but they were allowed to hold some positions of power depending on their history, affiliations, and experience. They were also able to own property, which was a recent change, and from what I was hearing was just the beginning as new bills were being championed by the Human Rights Transity. A global rights party that I followed and voted for in nearly every election process. There was still a lot of fear surrounding men rising to power again. It was the constant rallying cry of the Binary Purists and their political party: Women First.

A lot of times, you could only tell if someone had transitioned because of their height, and even then it was hard to tell because of years of gene manipulation. The necessary medical procedures were extensive but included in the Uniformity's Universal Healthcare, as it was not designated as an elective procedure. If it was necessary for your mental health, then it was covered. So perhaps "choice" was an antiquated phrase in regards to transitioning. Because really, when it came down to it, there was no choice. You could live your truth, or you could live in constant dysphoria. One path leads to happiness, the other to daily pain.

I watched Skyye continue to turn the pages as the women around her giggled and swapped war stories, previous arguments forgotten. Skyye was absorbed in the book, struggling to look nonchalant as she tuned out the women around her and absorbed herself in the pictures.

A particularly handsome specimen had her attention drawn longer than any other - a lightly muscled body, long dusty brown hair pulled back at the nape of his neck. The picture showed a defined figure, a light stubble and a bright laughing face. The picture boasted a full four gears. Skyye's hand shook as she turned the page.

I memorized the menu number, in case she forgot it.

Charlene, the woman who had been balancing on the stage not moments ago, chose then to come take drink orders. She scurried quickly away without a sound as soon as she was done.

Skyye flipped through the next few pictures without really looking at them, then switched to focus on the female menu.

It was much the same, but without the gear rating. It would be pointless to rate what you could see. Women of all shapes and sizes graced the pages. Pin-up poses dominated the style of pictures, as they all looked their sexiest. Skyye paused at a traditional kimono-wearing geisha. She sat at a tea table, back straight and poised, pouring tea with two hands. Dainty saucers and cups with cherry blossoms graced the table, making the scene look very welcoming.

"Did you find one you like dear?" Josephine asked her.

"I think so," Skyye blushed prettily, and I felt a squeeze in my gut for her.

"Do you want me to go with you to the bar?" Josephine asked.

"No!" Skyye said quickly, then recovered. "But thank you for offering."

Skyye jumped down from her seat and moved quickly to the bar with the leather-bound books. I watched to make sure she didn't forget the menu number but she seemed to place her order quickly, then came back without a second thought. Amadeus nodded, beaming, and sent me a thumbs up. I held back a laugh as she rejoined us.

"They are preparing a room," Skyye let out a breath, her

excitement beginning to show.

No longer was she the sullen teenager that had sat in my living room just an hour before.

Charlene came back with our beverages and left again without a word. The white face paint and black tears gave the impression she was indeed sad. On the stage now was Charlene's counterpart, who had white face paint and a large black smile. She wore nothing but a halo and white feathered wings.

Her breasts were proudly exposed to the crowd as she recited poems by Sylvia Plath, with what looked like blood running down her arms. The two were great performers, espousing the hidden demons many possessed. Their performances spoke of keeping things hidden that were unwelcome subjects to those around you.

Appropriately, the women around me talked amongst themselves and ignored the stage.

Soon enough, the woman in the kimono that we'd seen earlier in the catalogue came to our table.

"I heard it was someone's Deflowering tonight," she bowed deeply. "I am honored to guide you to your room."

"Thank you," Skyye stood, then smiled addressing the group. "I don't know how long I'll be, if any of you feel like leaving that's ok."

"I can make sure she gets home," I said to her grandmother Josephine before she could protest.

"That would be wonderful!" My mother responded enthusiastically. "Yes, let us leave and let her have her Deflowering. We old biddies don't need to hover. And we can find an establishment much more to our taste."

The ladies all nodded, so Josephine did as well. Josephine hugged her granddaughter and the rest moved back to the stairs. I waved goodbye and took my seat again.

"You ready?" I asked Skyye when we were alone.

She grinned happily.

"Good trick having someone else escort you to your

room," I winked and she blushed deeper. "Good luck."

Skyye walked around the table and hugged me hard. I was taken aback at first but I returned her embrace, then she broke away and skipped off to follow the woman in the Kimono. With that done I turned back to the bar, thinking about questioning Amadeus again.

But another had taken his place. Amadeus had gone home for the night.

 I found a smaller table and straddled a chair with my back to the wall. I'd paid for my group's abandoned drinks back at the bar, and asked the replacement bartender to confirm Amadeus had gone. He had.

The official response was that he came down with some sudden sickness. And though he had looked gaunt, there was something else. I could feel it. And though my back was to the wall, my skin continued to itch. I learned a long time ago to listen to my instincts. I watched the stage, not really registering what was happening there, but letting my periphery loosely watch the body language around me.

I checked the news updates on my wrist unit regularly, but the lack of incidents didn't make me feel better. I just kept replaying the man's face in my head.

Bump, turn, sharp blue eyes widen. Panic, turn away and disappear into the crowd.

Did they widen in recognition? How would he know me? If he was unaffected by The Scourge, why was he risking himself now? Everyone knew that some men could still contract The Scourge, even if they had been spared previously. The only safe place was their small patriarchal societies, untouched by the virus and modern technology.

His eyes were what haunted me most. That blue seemed familiar somehow. The longer I thought about it, pressed myself to recall, my head began to thump with my heartbeat.

I exhaled and pushed my beverage away, then pulled out a quick pain blocker from the small handbag I'd brought along to subdue my headache. I returned my attention to the stage as I waited for the pain reliever to kick in. Headaches and migraines were frequent. I could never figure out why, but sometimes they even had accompanying nose bleeds if I pushed myself.

My memory was precise. I remembered details years after the fact and could recall things easily. Most things anyway.

The headaches could get in the way sometimes.

All of the doctors I've seen about it have said that they couldn't find anything wrong and not to dwell on it. So I let it go.

A lounge singer was now gracing the stage, swaying back and forth while holding a microphone stand. Her sorrowful song plucked at my heartstrings, making my chest ache for something I couldn't put my finger on. The deep red dress she wore reflected the light with her movement, turning the immediate area into a small disco as she sang. The fabric moved easily and looked soft as it glittered lightly.

My headache began to ease as I listened. I let my eyes unfocus as the music flowed over me. Movement ahead of me snapped my attention back as I saw Skyye return from the same hallway she had disappeared down with the robed woman. Her cheeks were flushed as she seemed to float across the floor toward me. The dreamy look on her face made my night.

"So," I grinned at her. "How was it?"

"It was amazing," Skyye plopped down in the chair across the tiny table from mine and sighed deeply. "It was exactly what I wanted. He was sweet, and shy, but he knew exactly what he was doing."

"I'm glad," I checked my wrist unit. "Looks like you've been busy for about two hours."

"Really," Skyye blushed again. "I had no idea."

"That's exactly how it should be," I smiled and she swayed lightly to the crooning from the stage. The last thing I wanted to do was burst this happy little bubble, so I waited until the song was over before I asked.

"Are you ready to meet up with your grandma?"

"I suppose," Skyye looked longingly toward the hall she'd emerged from.

Just then the kimono wearing geisha appeared from the doorway and walked straight to us, bowing as she reached our table.

"I am happy to invite you to become a member," the woman held out a small business card to Skyye with a single word scrawled onto it. "Be sure to keep this password close to you, and do not share it. Your membership is revoked immediately if your password is used without your presence. On the back is the password to use if you bring someone to accompany you. At the time of use, your voucher to bring someone is voided and will be reissued again after one calendar year has elapsed. So choose wisely who to bring into GrandIloquence."

With another bow, she turned and left.

Skyye held the card reverently.

"You're in," I stood and pulled her up. "We should head out."

"You used your once a year password for me?" Her eyes watered.

I sent a signal to the bartender to wrap it up on my tab and we moved towards the exit.

"Of course kid," I grinned at her. "You needed it and were well worth the use."

I watched her tuck the card into an inner pocket and zip it closed.

I sent my mother a quick text via my wrist unit to ascertain their current location. She responded quickly. It was only a few blocks away.

I nodded to Violet on our way out.

"See you next week, Dekka?" Violet asked.

"More than likely," I waved and sent them a wink as I ushered Skyye out the door.

The heavy portal slid shut and clanged as the locks moved into place.

I listened to Skyye chatter about her experience. I made the appropriate noises so she knew I was paying attention, but I was still on-guard, watching my surroundings. When we reached the mouth of the alley my skin began to itch again. I slowed my walk, and held an arm out to slow Skyye as well, who'd grown quiet. My attention had been caught by something I couldn't yet solidify.

"Your grandma is just a couple blocks down, at Fancy," I touched Skyye's shoulder, interrupting what she was about to say. "I've got something to take care of, but I'll try and catch up later."

"Ok," Skyye seemed saddened by my announcement, but nodded. "Thank you again, really."

My lips curved upward as I looked at her for a moment.

"You're a woman," I told her. "Do what makes you happy, but remember what I told you."

Skyye nodded sadly then waved as she turned to find her grandma and the rest of her party. I watched her disappear down the street before I scanned the street again, which was mostly empty. I sent my mother a message to let her know that Skyye was on her way, but I would not be there as something had come up and that I'd explain later.

I turned in the opposite direction that Skyye had left by and I began walking. I moved quickly and turned into the shadowed enclave of a shop that was closed for the night. I crouched and waited. The night was silent and the street was lit like any other, but this specific street had a reputation for constantly having the street lights broken. This was part of why GrandIloquence could easily maintain its secret clientele. Minutes passed. There was no movement on the street and I cursed myself for being paranoid. The run-in earlier had triggered something, and I was seeing enemy operatives everywhere.

Just as I was about to stand I heard footsteps walking toward my position. I pressed my back into the wall, trying to make myself as small as possible. The footfalls grew closer and more hesitant, like they were looking for someone. I could tell by the sound that it was only one person, slight of build.

The target passed my location without looking into the dark enclave. The small amount of light on the street reflected off the white shirt with its sleeves rolled up, and black vest with a large gear sewn on the back.

Amadeus?

I slipped out behind him and let him continue on. He walked quietly and quickly as he scanned the street. I matched my steps to his and bided my time. Without the stilts his height was barely a meter and a half and I now towered over him. The moon was in front of us, so the light didn't cast my shadow ahead of him.

"Who are you looking for?"

Amadeus nearly fell over at the sound of my voice cutting through the silence.

"Dekka Casey," he whirled and squeaked. "I was looking for you."

His eyes darted around the empty street, then he motioned for me to follow him down another alley. Silently, we moved through a series of alleys and streets until we reached a small waterway. The hairs on the back of my neck began to stand on end and I paused, listening, as he disappeared down some stairs.

"What are we doing, Amadeus?" I called down the stairs.

"Shh!" Came a desperate hush from below.

I pulled a small clutch piece from my handbag, the metal cold in my hands. I surveyed the area again before descending the stairs.

A bridge shadowed the sidewalks of the irrigation canal and my eyes adjusted slowly as I entered the darker area. I saw Amadeus standing in the shadows of the bridge, motioning me closer.

I hit the bottom of the stairs and whipped around in the opposite direction, holding my weapon close but ready. The area was clear. I turned back to Amadeus, happy that I'd decided to wear my boots tonight instead of heels. I kept my weapon in my hand, relaxed at my side, as I approached the shadow of the bridge.

The water echoed here as it flowed in the canal next to the small walks, making the sound much louder as it bounced around under the bridge. Something occurred to me.

"Are you afraid I'm wearing a wire?" I lifted a brow as I finally reached him.

I turned my back to the cement wall and forced Amadeus to face me, his back to the canal. I leaned against the cool wall, affecting an air of being more casual than I felt. My weapon held loosely next to the wall in my left hand.

"This protects us both," Amadeus replied. "You know better than I that the Uniformity is always watching."

I shrugged. It was a well known myth that the Uniformity had cameras everywhere, and we didn't confirm or deny this. People tended to be on better behavior if they thought they were being watched.

"What are we doing?" I stage-whispered, a mock smile slid easily into place.

"You asked me a question tonight," Amadeus walked closer to me so that he could talk in a hushed whisper and still be heard.

I angled my weapon up between us, moving like I was just readjusting my position to hear him better.

"I did," I confirmed. "Do you have information for me?"

My eyes narrowed as I took in his body language.

He was nearly shaking with nerves. He knew that he was putting his job at risk by informing on a patron.

"You have my word I won't release your name in my report," I told him. "C.I.s are protected by the Uniformity, especially if their information leads to a Resistance Cell. I can tell you the current reward for an active cell is about two-years salary."

Amadeus relaxed visibly and the tension left my shoulders, though I stayed on guard.

"What did you see?" I prompted.

"A man," he stated quietly. "Untouched by Scourge. Unaccompanied. He met with Charlene before she went on stage tonight."

"What did he look like?" I asked.

"He..."

That was all I got before an enormous *BOOM* had me ducking down and Amadeus took off running.

"Hey!" I started to go after him, then looked over my shoulder to see what the sound had been. Orange and red danced in the night sky turning it purple in the distance.

Faint screaming could be heard in the distance and I could see the reflection of growing fires in the direction we'd come from.

"What in Hades?" I took off running toward the screams.

Sirens screeched as I ran toward the fire.

I could see lights in the sky as the hovercopters made their way through, using their spotlights to search the surrounding area.

Chaos erupted around me as I got closer to the incident site. Open-mouthed pedestrians stood around horrified, gaping at the destruction of what had been a HoPP just minutes before.

"Move back!" I yelled at the people who were watching the fires burning the once well-known establishment.

At my words, some shook themselves out of their stupor and began creating a perimeter with me. We moved back the rest of the bystanders a full block as the emergency vehicles made their way through. Hoses were hooked up and deployed with the ease of practice. Within fifteen minutes of the explosion, the blaze that had consumed the House was out.

"Casandra!" My mother's voice could be heard over the crowd that watched the horror.

I walked over and hugged her, glad that she was safe.

"Are you alright?" She demanded.

"I'm fine," I told her. "I was nowhere near here when it happened."

"It's a good thing our reservations were cancelled tonight," my mother stated. "Or this could have been the death of us."

"Hmm," I frowned, thinking about the coincidence of the past few hours and what had transpired.

"It's lucky you weren't near here either," she patted her chest where her heart lay, as if it were beating intently. "It seems like it happened while a performance was beginning down the street, so there weren't many people around the building either."

I needed to find Amadeus. Something told me he may be the key, or at least a piece of the puzzle.

"Skyye and the others went home," my mother continued. "But I needed to make sure you were safe."

"I'm fine," I repeated. "You should go home and get some rest. I'm gonna need to go in and report this incident tonight."

"Oh," she smiled and touched my shoulder. "Then I'll make my way home as well. Stay safe please."

"I will," I promised and hugged her again before she turned and moved through the crowd.

"Was anyone here a witness to what happened?" I yelled into the crowd.

A few tentative hands raised.

"I'll need you to move over to the left of the barriers so we can interview you," I announced to the crowd at large. "As soon as you answer a few questions, you can go home."

The chaplains that had been deployed to the area earlier, at my seemingly paranoid urging, followed my lead and began asking the same questions, corralling the witnesses. The crowd began to disperse as we carried out our jobs.

I could hear some of the other statements around me as we worked.

"I watched someone go in there right before the explosion," one person said. "White dress and blond hair."

"I saw a chaplain, yelling at a girl to get down off the fence earlier," another spouted.

I took notes and asked questions. My heart began to hurt.

When I was done with my witnesses, I asked the chaplains to copy their statements to my file so I could write up a report tonight as first on scene.

Another Dekka was making their way through the crowd, looking tired and worn.

"Dekka Marlon," I nodded to them as they approached me.

"Dekka Casey," she smiled wanly. "What do we have here?"

I gave her a quick rundown to bring her up to speed and promised to send her a copy of my report as soon as I finished it, as she was the one on call, she would need to submit it in tandem with her own findings.

"There are a few chaplains still working on wit statements, but the majority have been seen and dismissed," I finished.

"What the hell happened?" Marlon turned toward the smoking wreckage.

"Unclear," I shook my head. "But I think when all is said and done we will have at least a couple of casualties on our hands. Including a girl trying to sneak in for her Deflowering."

Marlon sighed and rubbed her temples.

"Almost off shift?" I asked because it looked like she hadn't slept.

"I was just about to hand off when I got the call."

"Bum deal."

"You're telling me," Marlon looked me up and down. "If you weren't so good with the recruits and sussing out the leaders, I'd be jealous of your bank hours. But I don't want your job."

I cocked a brow and let that slide.

"I'll send that copy," I repeated before waving off and heading toward my own home.

Some small aches and pains were beginning to make themselves known, but the night wasn't over yet. Looks like I'd be hitting up GrandIloquence again much sooner than I'd anticipated.

****

Unsettling colors surrounded me. Reds, pinks, yellows. They suffocated me with their brightness.

I fought against something pinning me down. When I was able to open my eyes, the laser blue burned into mine.

"Who are you?!"

No answer. I shut my eyes to block out the colors, but they exploded behind my lids like fireworks.

I heard a scream. I was running. I wasn't pinned anymore.

Was I running to, or from? Did someone need help? Did I need help?

There was a man in front of me, but I couldn't see his face. He was there, then he wasn't. It was like a computer glitch. His movements were lagged and he teleported around an unfamiliar room.

Talking, yelling, pleading.

A gear was flying through the air.

No, it was swinging like a pendulum.

I could feel something in my hands, its fibers burned through my skin like fire.

Friction.

I watched the light leave the eyes in front of me, but they weren't blue anymore. I squeezed the snake in my hands and it bit my palms with its fire.

"CAS!" The voice was wrong.

The blue eyes were back, they floated in front of me, mocking.

"Stop fighting" they said without a mouth. *"You won't remember anyway, so just hold still and you'll forget."*

A scream ripped through the air, this time I knew it was mine.

I sat up in the darkness, cold sweat pouring down my spine.

It's been a long time since I've had a nightmare like that. They were never the same, except for those eyes.

Maybe that was why they'd stood out to me on the street. They couldn't have been the same, though.

I stretched out on my bed around oh-six-hundred.

The night had been long and I was finally able to crawl into bed after I finished reviewing my notes and writing my report. I sent it to Dekka Marlon and copied it to my superiors before heading to bed. I breathed deep the soft scent of my pillow and began to drift off.

I grunted when my wrist unit began to signal.

Blearily I looked at the readout and sighed, closing my eyes again as I accepted the transmission. Audio only.

"Yes?" I answered.

"Where are you?" Came the demanding tone I wished I could forget.

"I'm in bed, Victoria," I attempted to keep the disdain from my voice, but some must have slipped through.

"There's no need to take that tone with me," Victoria hissed. "You're late for your classes."

"What are you talking about," I cracked open an eye to study my wrist unit again. "It's Saturday."

My eyes widened as I shook my wrist unit, as if that would correct the date.

"It's Monday and you very well know it," Victoria growled. "What, did you have too much fun over Centennial weekend? Black out or something?"

"Or something..." I muttered into my pillow, my unit read Monday, oh-eight-thirty.

Did I sleep for forty-eight hours?

"What was that?" Victoria nearly screeched.

"Nevermind, just get your ass to work."

"Look Victoria," my mind reeled as I tried to remember

anything from the past two days. "I'm really not feeling well. I'm sorry, but I'm going to have to call in sick."

I tucked my wrist unit under my pillow as a resounding screech came through the unit. I left it there, listening for the end of her muffled rant.

"I'll get someone to cover my afternoon classes," I said as soon as she took a breath. "Apologize to the recruits for me."

I ended the transmission and continued to stare at my wrist unit. My stomach did flips and my mouth ran dry. I didn't feel bad about calling out sick. I haven't used a single sick day since I started with the Academy three years ago. I pushed away the exhaustion I felt and threw my legs over the side of the bed.

I stumbled toward my bathroom, but hit a wall in the darkness.

"Ouch," my head pounded. "Lights on, twenty percent."

The lights didn't respond and the darkness continued.

"Fuck," I fumbled along the wall for the switch, and hit it when I found it. I wasn't used to using the switch manually. The lights burned my eyes, so that I was blinded for a moment. Then I felt the blood leave my face and I felt dizzy. This was not my bedroom.

This was not my bedroom and a body hung from the rafters, neck bent awkwardly from the rope attached at their throat. My hands burned, remembering the nightmare fibers burning into my palms. Had it been a dream?

A familiar white shirt and black vest with a gear on the back shined in the light.

I found the restroom just in time to lose whatever I'd eaten, though judging from the mainly acid and dry heaving it hadn't been much.

I wanted to scream but I clamped down on the urge and let my training take over. Whatever had happened, I needed to make sure my presence was scrubbed from the scene. I flushed the mess I'd made and began looking around, cataloging my surroundings. The mint green bathroom was badly out of date, and filthy. I resisted the urge to vomit again as I gagged. I moved to the mirror in order to assess myself. It was small, but if I moved around I could see most of myself.

I was wearing nothing but a pair of panties, but I couldn't remember if those were the ones I'd gone to bed in.

The last thing I remembered was coming home, showering, finishing my report, and then falling into bed. I'd looked at the digital clock on my nightstand before I shut my eyes. So I know it had been 0600. Now it was 0815 on Monday.

I turned and found some dark yellowing bruises on my side, like I'd taken blows at least twenty-four hours ago. As I tried to bring the memories back, my brain felt like it was full of angry bees and began pounding heavily.I looked closer at my arm as I saw bruised spots in an odd pattern on my arm. I turned to the side and ran my hand over the markings. As I did, I realized it fit the pattern of fingers, big ones. Larger than my own hand.

Someone had grabbed me hard enough to leave a mark and I didn't remember it.

I jumped as my wrist unit signaled.

"Hello?" I asked without checking the readout as I continued to study my body.

"Oh, thank the Goddess," came the answer.

"Mom?"

"I've been trying to get a hold of you all weekend!" She scolded. "Where have you been?"

"That's the question of the hour," I said to myself.

"What?" My mother asked, confused.

"Nothing, mom," I shook myself. I badly wanted to grab for the bottle of blockers on the counter as my headache ratcheted up to an eight. But judging by the body in the other room, I needed to limit my exposure to my surroundings. At the very least, I was now a part of a crime scene. "Why do you ask?"

"You know why," she sounded impatient. "You barged

into my house Saturday evening spouting nonsense. Then you..."

Her voice trailed off.

"Then I?" I prompted.

She sighed.

"I need to see you," was all she said.

"I'm not really feeling well, mother," I told her honestly.

"You need to see something," she said urgently. "Something tells me it's important."

"Alright." I frowned again at the marks ranging across my body. I'd been in multiple fights. And now there were cuts through the tattoo on my shoulder, as if someone had tried to erase the name. "I'll head over as soon as possible."

"Good," my mother seemed relieved. "I'll see you soon."

"See you," I ended the transmission. I doubted it would be soon.

I sent off a quick message to a peer officer in recruitment to cover my classes for this afternoon, tomorrow, and potentially the rest of the week. I pushed through the panic that was setting in. I could let myself go later. This wasn't like the experiences where I'd lost time while I attended University.

I couldn't have done this. I needed to erase my presence here as quickly as possible. I located cleaning supplies under the sink and began to wipe down every surface. I even wiped down the rope, though I did so without directly looking at it, because I knew what would happen if I was ever placed at the scene.

A memory download. They weren't perfect, but I knew there was a loophole. It had been exploited by enough people to get out of trouble that it called into question the dependability of evidence obtained from someone's mind. If you didn't look directly at something, it could be interpreted in many different ways. So I avoided looking directly at the body and the rope.

There was no way to know what surfaces I'd touched.

When I finished with the bathroom, it glistened better than it probably had in a decade. Using a garbage bag I gathered the garbage and anything else that might contain my DNA as I went, continuing to look for clues, then moved to the bedroom.

I found a pair of jeans that weren't too big and an oversized t-shirt to put on. I longed for my normal clothes and wondered what had happened to them. They were a moveable fabric and moisture wicking, which is why they were standard issue across all levels. It made it easy to decide what to put on everyday.

As much as I wanted to I couldn't look at Amadeus as he hung silently, watching my journey through the room, but I knew it was him. His feet were bare and I pinched a purple swollen toe to judge the rigidity. He'd probably died at least twenty-four hours ago.

I moved to the bed and stripped the sheets, and shoved them with the pillows into a second garbage bag. I didn't worry about the body because I'd seen him when he was alive, so there was plausibility if my fingerprints or DNA would be found on him. When I was finished a little under an hour had passed, and in any other situation I would have congratulated myself.

I let myself look up at what had been Amadeus for one second and then I looked away. His blank eyes were filmed with death and I wondered again what had happened. There wasn't a chair or ladder or anything that would have been needed if this was suicide. The ceiling wasn't low enough that he could have tied himself up there. He'd had help.

When downloading memories, they never played like a movie. There were scene jumps and erosion as time passed any event in question. Without knowing exactly what you were looking for, memories were nearly impossible to decipher. They were most helpful if the event was traumatic or important to the holder, because they were much clearer to view.

I threw the two bags over my shoulder and consulted my wrist unit using the GPS to locate where I was. I was downtown, not too far from my row house. I plotted my course mentally through back streets. I knew I would stick out like a sore thumb with not one, but two garbage bags. No one had this much trash, ever. I needed to move quickly, but running with the trash would look even worse. I couldn't wait any longer, or there would be more people on the street as early lunches and shift changes began.

I took a deep breath and walked out the door without a backward glance. I walked up the stairs of the basement unit, fixed a confident look on my face and walked farther down the alley and onto the back streets as if I belonged there.

I moved quickly, but I didn't jog like I normally would.

When I reached my house, I stripped as soon as I stepped in the back door. I shoved those clothes and my underwear into the garbage bags and left them in my kitchen. I very nearly ran up the stairs to my own bathroom. I downed two blockers with shaking hands from my vanity, and drank water until my stomach sloshed.

I needed an incinerator. Good thing I knew where to find one, but first I needed to take a shower.

I stepped into my stall.

"Water, ninety degrees."

The water cascaded over my head and I let myself go for a moment. There was sound proofing throughout my home. I let the anguish, confusion, and anger spill out of me. I screamed like I'd wanted to before. Tears hotter than the water I stood under flowed from my burning eyes. A beep from above told me it had been five minutes and the water would be shutting off soon. I quickly washed away my pain and the dirt from my sore body, then stepped out to mechanically dry off.

Bruises, newer than the ones on my sides, covered the inside of my thighs. An unknown shame washed over me as I realized there was a soreness between my legs as well.

What had happened to me? I began to feel hopeless as I walked into my room and saw my bed. I wanted to crawl beneath the covers and never emerge. The adrenaline that had been pushing me since I was woken by Victoria faded, and left my knees weak.

To my unending shame, I nearly gave in then. Nearly.

I moved to my safe, breathing a sigh of release as I saw everything was there. I pulled out my weapon, thigh harness and ID. Once I was strapped, I turned to close the safe and realized something *was* missing.

My clutch piece.

I walked to my closet and found the handbag that I'd carried Friday night, but no weapon. I did a quick walk-through of my room and the apartment but I didn't see anything. I knew I'd brought it home with me. I double checked the night stand next to my bed, just in case. Nothing.

A feeling of dread settled in my stomach. What if I'd missed it at the crime scene? It would point directly back to me. Every weapon was registered. I would need to report it missing, and I wasn't even sure *when* it went missing.

I walked down the stairs, grabbed the garbage bags, and down another set of narrow stairs in the kitchen that lead to the basement garage.

"Lights on full," I ordered, and the lights responded as they should. I had a two person all terrain vehicle and a light motorbike for personal use. I didn't use them often, but I kept them for long distance journeys.

I tossed the bags into the trunk, and then slipped into the driver's seat, ignoring the sweat on my palms. I pressed the garage door opener and slid out onto a nearly empty street. Those neighbors that recognized me waved, and I waved back, faking the cheer I knew I would have if I were driving for the first time in a while. I watched the garage doors close behind me, then turned my thoughts to what was ahead of me.

Since it wasn't far, I began driving toward

GrandIloquence first.

The morning was bright and sunny with a crispness in the air that made it comfortable to run in. I rolled down my window to feel the breeze on my face as I drove. I could feel a cold sweat running down my back as my muscles screamed against the safety belt and any small movement. I pushed through the pain. I couldn't remember the last time I felt this sore. Even after days of matches, taking hits and returning for more.

I did my best not to panic, but my chest was tight and I was having a hard time breathing.

When I reached the mouth of the alley that contained the establishment, I parked in an open spot nearby and sprinted to the doorway. Now well lit in the daytime, the alley looked like any other. I knocked and gulped in the air as I waited.

The metal peephole slid with a screech. Tired, bleary eyes stared back at mine.

"Violet," I breathed.

"Dekka," Violet greeted slowly. "What brings you here this time of day?"

"Let me in," I told her. "I need to speak to anyone that was here over the weekend."

"Password?" Violet's eyes narrowed.

"Marqué," I ground out. "Look this is an emergency."

"That's not your password," Violet began to close the slot.

"Wait! What do you mean?"

"I..." Violet seemed conflicted. "You changed your password this weekend."

"No I didn't," I frowned.

"You changed it with me," she prompted as if begging me with her eyes to remember. "You were very specific about the word and to not allow you entrance unless..."

"Unless?" I demanded.

"Unless you spoke the new password," Violet answered. "I'm sorry, you told me even if you forgot it that I couldn't allow you entrance. You made me give you my word."

With that, Violet shut the peep.

I yelled and pounded on the door in my frustration.

"What the hell is going on?!" I growled.

I turned back toward the mouth of the alley, jumped into my car and began my trek to my mother's. After what seemed like an eternity, I arrived at the gate to my family's estate.

It was just outside of the city and it sprawled across twenty acres of forested land. I punched in the code at the gate, slipped through as soon as it was wide enough and sped my way up the drive. The trees and bushes that lined the driveway were beginning to hibernate. Some stubborn pink blooms hung on for dear life, even as their sisters withered and died around them.

My mother's mansion rose high above me as I approached. Beautifully crafted stone pillars matched the tan brick of the facade. Accented by white trim, it looked elegant and stately, just as my mother had intended.

As I began climbing the stairs to the arching front entrance the doors were thrown open and my mother ran out.

"Casandra!"

I jumped out of my car and limped up the wide sprawling stairs toward her.

"Mom, I think I'm in trouble," I tried to say, but the bees in my head took over and I don't think I got all the words out.

"Daily!" I heard my mother yell. "Daily, help!"

I pitched forward as I tripped on the final stair, expecting to hit my head hard.

When the pain didn't happen, I tried to focus on my surroundings. I realized I was floating.

No, I wasn't floating. I was being carried.

There was no way my mother could carry me in her arms this way. I looked up to see a square jaw and sharp blue eyes.

"You," was all I could get out, before darkness claimed my reality and I lost consciousness.

Not you, anyone but you.

 Warmth surrounded me. I floated on a cloud, safe and secure.

I could hear voices raised in irritation, but I pushed them away. I didn't want to leave the warmth. It was so much more welcoming than what awaited me. I floated steadily on clouds the color of an early sunrise. Enveloped in pink I waited for someone just out of reach.

Jen.

The voices raised to near shouts and it became hard to shut them out.

"...did I tell you?" A deep voice chastised. "She's been reconditioned too many times."

"...couldn't be helped," another voice defended. "She knew what she was signing up for."

"...sign up for this?!?" The first voice elevated in octaves, making my head pound and buzz again.

"...waking up," the second voice said quietly.

"...have to go," the first said, a note of frustration touched the edges and I wondered why they were so angry.

The voices quieted and I was able to float away again. Searching for... something.

I opened my eyes in darkness. The green glow of the heart monitor was the only light in the room.

I tried to sit up and immediately regretted it. My right side screamed in pain and I could feel a warm wetness that suggested I'd pulled a stitch.

"Fuck?" I felt around my stomach and confirmed my suspicions.

I blindly moved my hands around the bed and only found blankets.

"Hello?" I called, but the only answer was the faint beeping of the monitor.

Without twisting too much I felt along the side of the bed

and found a glass of water. I picked it up and drank it greedily. My mouth was dry as a desert.

I could hear soft footsteps approaching my location. Tenderly, I tried to prop myself up. I could feel the bandages on my side soaking through, but I needed to be ready for whatever was coming.

When the lights flipped on, I squinted and blinked at the brightness. As my eyes adjusted, I saw my mother walking toward me with a tired and worried look on her face. I blew out a sigh of relief as my surroundings came in to focus.

"Casandra," she breathed. "How are you feeling?"

"Like I got run over by a truck," I looked around my childhood bedroom. "What the hell happened?"

"What do you remember?" She prompted.

"I..." My brain began buzzing angrily as I tried. "The last thing I remember is trying to get here. I got to the gate and it just goes blank." I decided to leave out the other parts of my missing memories. At least for now.

My mother closed her eyes and sighed.

"What happened?" I repeated, for the first time I was beginning to feel panic.

"There was an accident," she looked away as she spoke.

"What do you mean?" I demanded.

"Your townhome was the target of another attack," she said.

"What?" My mouth fell open.

"You left the estate after we talked and you were about to enter your house when there was an explosion." She paced away as she spoke.

"I don't..." I was at a loss. I couldn't remember any of that.

"You spent several days in the hospital, before I had them move you here so you could be more comfortable."

She turned back to me then and laid her head gently on my shoulder.

"I've been so worried."

"How..." I cleared my throat around the lump that had

formed there. "How long have I been asleep?"

"A few weeks."

"Weeks?" I croaked.

"You were very badly hurt," my mother sniffed as her tears began to dampen the gown I wore.

"I'm ok," I wrapped the arm I could lift around her without stretching the pain in my side, then I whispered in her ear. "Why are you lying?"

I had so many other questions, but they could wait. Finding out why my mother was feeding me lies, was the most important. I also knew she wouldn't lie for no reason. And that she was a very talented actor.

"I'm ok," I repeated again, loudly for the room as she began to sob, big wracking cries filled the silence.

I pulled her in closer and let it drop. I knew what she was trying to say.

I was being watched.

I began gaining information slowly through the orderlies, nurses, and doctors that came and went.

The Uniformity wanted to interview me about the attack as soon as possible, but my mother was holding them off. I wasn't sure what they were looking for, so it would be easy to fall into a trap.

I'd sustained surprisingly minor injuries for being as close to an explosion as they said. I had no burns, but I did have some road rash where the skin had torn after being knocked off my feet. I suffered a shrapnel impact though, which accounted for the deep wound on my left side.

The vague memories of voices when I'd been out of it seemed like a distant and unrealistic memory. What continued to bother me was the loss of time before I left for my mother's house.

My mother insisted that it was the attack that mixed up my memories, but something just didn't feel right. There were times my skin would itch at times when I laid in bed, alone. It itched the same way when I could feel someone watching me, or when my back was to a doorway. So I pretended like it didn't, until the feeling went away.

The day I was able to sit up without ripping any of my stitches was the day the Uniformity came calling.

"I told you," I could hear my mother saying from down the hall. "She's still in recovery."

"We won't stay long," a persistent voice came louder as they approached my door. "I'm sure Dekka Casey is eager to speak with us, as anyone in her situation would be."

Situation, I thought.

That was usually code for being under investigation. What did they know? Had someone seen me with trash bags?

Shit, the trash bags.

I could feel what color I had drain from my face.

"Dekka Casey," I recognized Dekka Marlon as she turned the corner and entered my room.

"Dekka Marlon," I nodded. "Thank you for taking the time to come to see me. I would get up..."

I let that hang in the air and her official smile dimmed just a little.

"How is your recovery?" She continued and pulled up a seat. "You don't look well."

She said that, as if she'd been expecting something else.

I noticed my mother hovering in the doorway.

"It's alright, mom," I sent her an encouraging smile. "This won't take long."

She hovered for a moment longer, then nodded and left.

"So what brings you to my recovery bed?" I asked, and made a decision. "You caught me on a good day, I was able to sit up today."

"We had some questions," Marlon pulled out a notepad and flipped through a few pages. "It seems there may be a few gaps in our information that you should be able to clear up."

"I'll do so to the best of my ability," I told her.

"As the Uniformity would expect," she pressed her middle and ring fingers to her lips and pointed to the ceiling.

"Exousia."

"Exousia," I mimicked the gesture, a formal greeting and ending when officially talking about the Uniformity.

It was a show of respect that carried through the last hundred years. People used to swear on things important to them, religious texts, documents of law. Now we swore on the Uniformity.

"They asked me to take your initial questioning," Marlon sighed. "Since we'd interacted just after the first incident at the HoPP."

"Logical," I nodded.

"So my first question stems from there," she continued. "After you left the scene with your notes and the compiled notes of the chaplains, you told me that you were going to go through all of the information, conduct a report and send it to me so that I could include it in my findings."

"Yes," I nodded.

"Why didn't you?"

"What do you mean?" I frowned.

"Why didn't you send me the report as you said you would," she repeated.

"I did," I told her. "I spent a few hours going over all the information and my own insights to create that report, then I sent it."

"What unit did you send it to?" She asked.

I opened my mouth to answer and my head began to buzz angrily.

"I can't recall," I stated. "But I know I sent it, right before..."

A slow dawning began to creep over me.

"Before..." Marlon prompted.

"I've been having some memory issues," I smiled apologetically. "Things seem to be hazy about the days leading up to the... incident at my home."

"I see..." Marlon jot notes and frowned. "Do you remember your whereabouts on Saturday?"

"I don't, I apologize," I sighed dramatically. "I'm just so angry that I must not have sent that report. I can tell you what I remember from that night. Would that help?"

The doctors would have already confirmed the amnesia, so this wouldn't come as a shock.

"It would," Marlon pursed her lips as she continued to write.

I laid out my steps and the locations we visited that Friday. I left out my meeting with Amadeus.

"You broke off from the group for a short amount of time before the HOPP incident," Marlon stated. "Where did you go?"

"Ah," I held my breath, while moving my chest to force my cheeks red as if I were embarrassed and breathing normally. "I went to visit a paramour."

"That's nothing to be ashamed of," Marlon frowned.

"Not if it was a woman," I took a deep breath and let it out. "I will answer any questions you have about it, but I would prefer to keep my predilections quiet if we can."

"Predilections?" Marlon sat forward.

My eyes darted to her chest, where I knew we all wore body cameras when on duty. Marlon understood and turned it off.

"I can't promise that this won't be in my report," she told me.

"I know," I left my eyes open so that they glazed a bit, looking watery. "I just need to make sure it's eyes only. It's...damaging..."

"Damaging?" Marlon's brows lifted up under her bangs at my use of the word.

Not many things were damaging to one's reputation.

"I have a weakness," I continued.

"We all do," Marlon said.

"But mine is..." I paused. "More than frowned upon."

"Ok," Marlon listened. "This is a safe space."

"I often go to clubs of a certain nature," I told her. "The

kind where pain and pleasure can be synonymous."

"That isn't shameful," Marlon relaxed and sat back a bit.

"No, of course not," I took another deep breath and paused. "Unless you were the one receiving pain and demands from a male."

Marlon's mouth fell open.

"And enjoying it," I buried my face in my hands. "I've been meaning to report it, to go in for reconditioning. But I'm addicted. I need help."

I pressed hard against my eyes so they would be red and watery when I dropped my hands.

"But you're our strongest Hoplomachos," she said aghast. "You eat lesser Dekkas for breakfast and go toe-to-toe with Lokhagos. You're infamous for your silent and quick attacks. I mean you're the *Sidewinder*. How can you let a *man* debase you that way. Let him *Dominate* you."

I let a single tear drift down my cheek, keeping my eyes downcast.

"I'm sorry that I've lost your respect," I breathed. "Do you understand now, why I need this to stay quiet? My reputation will be ruined. I'll be expunged."

"I see," Marlon re-engaged her body camera. "So you went to visit a...friend at another club before meeting up with your group again."

I nodded at her explanation, knowing that she would keep the lie a secret. Guilt washed over me, and I let the emotion stay in my eyes as I looked up. She knew that I would owe her after this. And owing someone, especially when keeping a secret of this magnitude was dangerous. But not as dangerous as the truth.

"And you've been indulging in activities that are..." She paused to find the right words. "Less than ideal for your health and mental stability."

I nodded.

"Well," Marlon stood. "That is all I need for now. When you're up for it, we will need to scan your memories to corroborate your movements."

"Of course," I smiled my thanks, even as my insides went cold as ice.

"If you remember anything else," Marlon took a card from her breast pocket. "Let me know immediately."

"I will," I said. "Thank you."

Dekka Marlon left as quickly as she'd come and I hoped that she bought the show. I waited until I heard the soft steps of another person approaching.

"Mother," I called.

"Yes dear," she answered and poked her head in and I beckoned her closer.

"Care to enlighten me as to why I just lied to the Uniformity?" I said quietly as she arrived at my bedside, looking like she was hiding something.

"I don't know what you're talking about," my mother, pulled back, sniffled and picked invisible lint off the shoulder of her blazer.

"I think you know exactly," I frowned at her.

"I have to go finish preparing for the charity auction," she stated. "It's to help rehabilitate what used to be Yellowstone Park. Which as you know was turned into an oil excavation site during the Unnamed administration."

"Is there a reason for this history lesson?" My head began to ache terribly and I rubbed at my temples.

"I just wanted you to know why you wouldn't see me for a day," she sighed. "Now, if you'll excuse me, I need to direct the staff."

"But..." She turned and left before I could finish my thought, or ask about the trash bags. Though the fact that the investigator didn't ask about them meant they hadn't been found yet.

A nurse came in with a plate of food and a tray to set it over my lap. He handed me a remote and left as quickly as my mother did.

The bed I was laying on was large enough to fit several people on it comfortably. I lay on the side closest to the door, for ease of access.

I'd grown up in this room and yet it continued to feel unfamiliar to me. A soft green colored the walls. The entire first floor of my apartment could fit in this one room. I'd chosen not to take any money from my mother to find a larger place to live, or for any other reason. I could afford the place I lived on my own salary, and it was more than enough room for me. I didn't need much.

The workforce that had been created by the Uniformity was a lesson in equity. Your salary was based on your years of experience and merit. The salaries weren't the draconian money concept that the world had capitalized and taken advantage of their laborers. There was no such thing as money in the traditional sense of capitalism. The work you did, reflected your lifestyle.

The Uniformity controls all jobs, so equity was across the board in every posting. There were extra incentives to motivate the highest level of commitment to the position. There were additional vacation days, though the base time off was four weeks for every position, and they never expired. The workforce was cross-trained in a minimum of two positions that were adjacent to their own, so that meant it was easy to flex for people to take time off. And no one had to worry about losing the position they were hired for, because it was easy to flex back.

Food, utilities, and power were already provided by the uniformity so money was unnecessary. Everything was based on a point system, the closer your job was to helping others the more points your salary was worth. So when you went to frequent luxury establishments like a restaurant, you used points to purchase things that aren't necessary for survival, but were good for morale.

I couldn't imagine the stress that the population under capitalism must have taken to function. Not knowing whether you could feed yourself, even though you were working back breaking hours.

I looked at the flaky crust of the croissant and mused about the differences in my life from birth to the present. I'd grown up with a silver spoon shoved in my mouth and it was kept there forcibly, until I was finally able to spit it out. There was still a pocket of wealthy matriarchs, and they usually worked in jobs that were charity outreach. Though there weren't social problems to remedy anymore like: homelessness, hunger, and victims of war; there were still scars on the earth that needed to be healed from hundreds of years of pollution, fracking, over-population, and lack of social programs. Not to mention the small resistance cells of those who did not want to follow us into the future. But the pockets of rebels held nothing of a candle to the previous war machines that raged across the world, so they didn't garner much attention.

Though my mother was one of them, it just seemed an odd premise. Homelessness, disease and hunger had been eradicated, but I couldn't help but wonder at times.

At what cost?

I shook away these thoughts and frowned. I hadn't been this introspective in a long time. I knew why our society operated the way it did. If anyone worked hard enough, they would contribute to their own wealth of points as well as their family's. Everyone had a job, no one wanted for anything. Why, suddenly, were these questions infiltrating my mind?

I understood and accepted how the Uniformity was created, why it existed, and why it needed to continue to do its work. Questions were answered, not deflected. Our society didn't expect you to buy into it with blind faith. Everything was logically and scientifically proven to work. Our current standing was proof of that.

I'd helped and worked within the Uniformity for years. I'd sacrificed a lot in the name of Peace and Prosperity.

My rational brain knew all of this.

But why was my chest feeling tight? Why was I reflexively grasping at the warm blankets around me? I felt like I was falling and didn't know when I would hit bottom. The events that I *could* remember were weighing on me, and the gaping black holes in my memory were the water that was closing in around me.

I picked up the tea from the tray, on its flowered saucer. It rattled in my hands as they shook. I focused on my breathing and smelled the humid floral scent, which slowed my quickly beating heart.

As I sipped the tea, my nervous system began to calm and the confusion I felt slipped away. Everything would work out. Whatever was going on, would be untangled.

Being in the dark was deeply uncomfortable, but I needed

to trust. My mother was hiding something and I needed to get down to the bottom of it. However, I knew that she would never do anything to hurt me.

I set the tea cup aside and pushed back into the pillows to gain more comfort. I yawned as I let my thoughts wash over me like an ebbing tide.

I would need to question my mother again about her involvement, and the whereabouts of the trash bags. The vague memory of someone mentioning reconditioning while I was sleeping haunted me slightly, but that could have been a nightmare created by my wounded mind.

Redaction tactics were rumored to have been used early on to gain compliance from a small minority around the change in hierarchy, mainly on men. Now, Redaction wasn't sanctioned under any circumstances, except in reconditioning. It was an invasive cranial procedure that rewrote, replaced, or removed memories through the hippocampus. Synthetic stem cells were used to create a bridge over the targeted memory, then cauterized so that it could be by-passed.

I laughed lightly at the thought of the Uniformity erasing memories whenever they wanted. As if I were some tin-foil hat wearing conspiracy theorist. The gaps in my memory could be from a traumatic brain injury. I fell asleep with the sound of my own laughter in my ears.

When I woke, I stretched and yawned. I had a nagging feeling that I was missing something, but I brushed it away. I pulled the blanket down and lifted my sleep shirt to see my bandages.

Running my fingers along the soft gauze, I pulled at the tape to see underneath. Pink and puckered, the Nu-Skin held my wound together. It itched horribly, but instead of giving in I put the tape back in place. I hadn't been injured often on the job before, beyond minor wounds.

I pulled down my nightshirt and slowly moved my legs over the side of the bed. I needed to move. I was no longer hooked up to the monitors so they sat, silent and dark, in the corner of the room.

Orange light glowed from the window opposite the door, casting the room in long shadows. I could hear faint music from below as I stood and remembered my mother talking earlier about some charity auction she'd been preparing for. Was that supposed to be today?

I frowned as I attempted to stand for the first time on my own in weeks.

My legs felt sore, but surprisingly steady. Cautiously, I walked to the door without incident. The hallway was empty, so I walked directly across to the bathroom, which connected to my wardrobe as well. I had left the majority of my clothes here since the closet in my apartment was small compared to this room, and I rarely wore anything other than my standard issue.

The bathroom was a study in luxury and I smiled at the familiarity of the white granite floors. Rather than cold, they were warm and comforting. One thing I did miss from this house was its use of heated tile, so your feet were never cold.

A double vanity dominated the left side of the wall, with a cushioned seat between the two deep bowl sinks serving as a powder area. To the right was a jetted tub the size of a small pond, which I knew I could stretch out in and not touch the opposing walls at the same time. The idea of floating sounded ideal at the moment, but slowly brought back the sounds of male voices that I couldn't quite place. I frowned as I closed and locked the door behind me.

My head began to buzz as I pushed at my recall and walked into the wardrobe room.

Ostentatious, the room could have housed my entire bedroom at my town home. It stretched deep and narrow, with a few cushioned seats if you needed to sit to try on shoes, or just to keep yourself from fainting from the sheer volume of clothes and accessories.

The clothes hung on revolving racks by color and rose

three racks tall, with a helpful rolling ladder to access them. There were six sections, three on the left wall and three on the right. The wall at the far end housed the shoes. Each was displayed with their heels touching, the left shoe facing the entrance and the right facing the left wall. Again they were sorted by color, each pair in their own backlit cube that measured point-three meters cubed, and the whole structure rose twenty cubes high. I could stand on my own head four times and maybe reach the ceiling.

There was a database linked to my wrist unit, and also conveniently to a touch pad on the wall for the use of the staff. If my mother asked a staff member to lay out a specific outfit for me it could be found and selected easily. Each section and hanger were labeled by color and position.

There was a small set of drawers, almost hidden on the walls next to the doors that housed what I was looking for. Underwear and a new sleep shirt. I knew I'd be in trouble if I tried to get dressed.

I opened the top drawer, selected panties at random then closed it. Then I opened another drawer and followed the same routine for a clean sleep shirt. As I was closing the drawer a duffel tucked under the first revolving rack on the ground caught my attention.

There was a separate section for luggage, which was kept in a couple of retracting shelves between the revolving racks. I frowned as I moved to pick it up. A sharp pain in my side had me hissing and standing upright again, but the quick movement had me light headed and shutting my eyes until the vertigo ended.

I eyed the duffel as I held my side. Deja Vu hit me and I nearly doubled over again when the angry buzzing in my head turned into stinging. I dropped the clothes I held to clutch my head.

I saw myself holding the bag behind my back. I was yelling something at my mother and she had tears streaming down her face, begging, pleading. But I couldn't hear what we were saying over the screaming bees in my head. Then it was gone and I was left in the shower, panting on the ground.

In the shower?

I still wore my sleep shirt, but now it clung to my body while water cascaded from the rain heads on the ceiling. My hair was soaked and the water ran cold. I sputtered as my body began to shake and I gingerly pushed up from the ground. The sheen of water over the dark marble of the tile floor seemed to mock me with my own reflection. When I was finally standing I moved the lever that controlled the temperature of the water so that it began to warm.

I waited until the shivering stopped then carefully removed my sodden sleep shirt and dropped it on the floor with a *plop*. I then turned my attention to the bandage on my side. Wet bandages were always hard to remove.

I breathed in a grunt as some of the Nu-Skin caught as I pulled it down slowly. Once it was removed I dropped it on the ground as well, and stepped out of my panties.

With a sigh I began to wash the sweat and sedentary lifestyle from my body. I turned the lever to the off position and stepped carefully out of the shower. There was no door or ledge, so that made it easier. Rather than risk snagging the Nu-Skin with a towel, I stepped into the drying tube next to the shower and raised my arms over my head. The warm air coursed over my skin and I was dry in a matter of moments.

I pulled my hair back into a short tail and walked back into my wardrobe to find my abandoned clothes. Carefully, I picked them up and my eyes sought the duffel and its distressed leather. But it was gone. I walked to the laundry chute and dropped the clothing into the darkness

I frowned as I dressed and walked to the wardrobe door. It was locked, as I'd left it when I entered. I left it locked and walked back into the room and searched through the luggage racks. Nothing.

My body was exhausted from the amount of activity it hadn't seen in a few weeks, but I pressed on. There had to be an explanation. I refused to believe I was going crazy.

When my search yielded no results, I thought about finding my mother. She knew what was going on and I needed answers. I remembered music coming from below and knew I would need to wear something a bit more acceptable to potentially be seen in public, rather than the sleep shirt I'd chosen.

I doubted I would be able to avoid everyone, and my reputation was still important to me. So even though I barely had the energy, I needed to push myself.

I slipped off the clean nightshirt and returned it to the drawer I'd found. Knowing my preferred clothes wouldn't be hung, I opened the next two drawers to find my standard black tank top and compression capris. Once I had those on, I walked back across the wardrobe, opened the locked door to my room in order to find my weapon, harness, and wrist unit.

There was a small wall safe next to the bed, where I assumed it had been stored. I put in my combination and the door popped open, but it was empty.

Feeling deeply uneasy I applied pressure to my side, which was beginning to throb, and began my trek down to the kitchens.

I felt naked without my weapon. My mother knew better than to hide it from me, and the procedure for a downed officer and their weapon. So the only logical explanation was that it had either been confiscated, or worse, I lost it in the blast.

I walked to the doorway that led to the hall. There were three stairwells that led downstairs. The one at the end of the hall in my wing led to the library. It was a favorite place of mine growing up. Limping a bit now, I went left down the hall to the adjoining wing. The doors all stood open as they were empty at the moment. Fresh linens would be gracing the beds so as to accommodate anyone who'd become too inebriated to leave until morning, which happened more often than anyone would expect at these functions my mother hosted.

I passed the main staircase that separated the wings and continued down the hall. No one had been inhabiting the grand foyer, but I could hear laughter from down below. Finally, I reached the end of the hall and walked down the stairs, gripping the railing as my legs were aching more with every step.

Reaching the bottom, I watched the kitchen staff running around. It was like an intricate ballet of plates and platters, swinging above and below others. They left the kitchen full and returned empty only minutes later.

I searched the faces for my mother, hoping I wouldn't have to track her down in the ballroom. There were times she escaped the ruthless droning of these events by hiding in the kitchen under the guise that something had been wrong with a plate, though nothing ever actually was because she'd trained the staff personally.

She wasn't here. I sank to the bottom step and sat as I watched, hoping she'd come in soon.

"Miss Casandra!" One of the staff rushed over when he saw me. "You shouldn't be down here."

His face, full of worry, darted back and forth as he searched the room for something.

"I'm looking for my mother," I tried to brush him off and stand, but my side started to scream. With a grunt I fell back onto the step.

"I'll go get her," he rushed out the door and came back with my mother in tow. Her hair was pulled up into a lavish coiffure and she wore a maroon evening gown, fitted hip to calf with a flair outward like a mermaid's tail.

"Casandra," a scowl was my greeting. "What are you doing out of bed? And dressed?"

"I needed to talk to you," I stated meaningfully. "I have more questions from this morning."

"This morning?" Her brows lifted and her mouth pursed as she thought. "I've been so busy with this event I haven't spoken to you in nearly a week."

"A week?" I shook my head. "The Dekka was just here this morning."

"No," my mother's brows tilted in concern. "Sweetheart that was days ago. Are you feeling ok?"

"Yeah," my stomach turned with the lie. "I'm fine. Come find me when the event is over. Sorry to bother you."

I stood slowly and began my long walk up the stairs again.

"Do you need any help?" My mother called after me.

"No," I waved her off. "I can do it."

My mind whirled as I climbed and my stomach was doing back flips. A sick terror had cold sweat soaking my skin. I needed to get to the bottom of this quickly, before I lost time again.

 I was panting by the time I'd reached the top and had the urge to just lay down right there. Instead, I focused on controlling my breathing .

On legs made of rubber, I began walking down the hall, back toward my bedroom.

I knew I'd pushed myself to the limit, but I needed answers. I refused to believe I was losing my mind. It was the only thing that I'd ever been able to rely on. So the idea that it was failing was not just terrifying, but unacceptable. I wouldn't allow it.

Using the wall for leverage I put one foot in front of the other. When I passed the main staircase I nearly lost my balance, but kept to the back wall in case anyone happened to be looking up. I didn't need anyone thinking they had to rescue me.

Sheer willpower kept me on my feet as I finally reached my bedroom door and slipped bonelessly to the floor, my back against the wall. Maybe I should have taken the offered help.

I stared across the hall into the dark bathroom. The faint light from the wardrobe had shadows dancing on the tiled floor.

I frowned as I watched. No flickering lights existed in the wardrobe, so how were there moving shadows unless...

The quick shot of adrenaline from the realization had me standing again and moving slowly to the bathroom. I entered the darkened room and kept the light off so that I could see the shadows under the wardrobe door, which was now closed. I know that I'd left it open.

At my approach all movement in the room ceased. I froze, heart pounding, and stood next to the door. I stared at the break between the tile and doorway. It was just wide enough to let light out. And I knew there were no lights behind me to give away my position because I never turned the lights on in my room.

Patiently, I waited for more movement. Time passed slowly as I waited. The adrenaline that had fueled my journey across the hall was slowly but surely evaporating. As my legs were beginning to shake, I wondered if I'd seen anything at all.

I was just about to turn to leave when a shadow passed under the door. Without considering my weakened state or the fact that I was without my weapon, I slammed open the door, hoping to catch the intruder unawares. Instead, I smacked him with the door.

With a grunt he fell backward onto the ground and I pounced. I felt a tearing in my side at the movement, but I was blind with rage. All the fear and emotion I'd been pushing away came to the forefront as we struggled. Rolling across the floor, I was surprised by how strong he was, and how *large*. I tried to pin his arms over his head, but his forearms were muscled. If this had been a normal man, even in my weakened state I would have been able to dominate him easily.

With a grunt he turned me over again, this time settling between my legs so I couldn't easily gain leverage. He used his weight to hold down my hips with his. A shock ran up my system with the contact and we continued to grapple with our arms.

"Stop," the man begged. "You're hurting yourself."

The sound of his voice made me hesitate, and he was able to gain the advantage, pinning my arms above my head as I'd tried to do earlier.

I squinted against the light above my head and tried to see his face, but it was in shadow as the light shone directly into my eyes.

"Who are you?" I demanded.

A deep chuckle rumbled from his chest and I began fighting again.

"Ok, Ok," he pushed my arms back above my head and pushed harder against my hips with his.

I froze at the sensation as fire scorched up my spine and

burned low in my belly.

Seeing my reaction he froze and a blush I didn't need to force heated my cheeks. Even though I still couldn't see his eyes, I looked away.

"Why did you laugh?" I asked.

"Because even when the chips are down, you still command," the voice floated deep and familiar in my ears.

I shuddered at the sound and felt a pulse low, where he pinned my hips. A memory was trying to surface but my head began to pound so it drifted away. The only thing that I could glean was that it wasn't a pleasant one, despite the easy cadence of his speech which denoted some form of familiarity.

"Who are you?" I repeated, turning back to try and see his face again.

"I'm sorry," he said regretfully.

"Why?" The apology had taken me completely off guard.

Men didn't apologize unless presented with no other option. Especially men who'd never known the effects of The Scourge.

He dipped his head and laid his lips on my neck. The soft sensation drew a gasp from my mouth and I arched away.

How dare he?

Slowly, being careful to keep my arms pinned, he rose. Then he let go of my arms, turned, and ran from the room.

I lay there on the floor of the wardrobe for a long time. I felt the wet stain my side and winced as I attempted to move. Pain erupted from my stitches. I wasn't sure what to be more astonished by, the man who had the ability to overpower me or the fact that he'd apologized for it.

The floor was beginning to seem more and more comfortable the longer I lay there. My head began to float and my eyes drifted closed, but I tried to keep them open. I didn't want to forget and I didn't want to lose more time.

I heard the soft thud of running feet coming down the hall as the darkness closed in around me again. I was terrified to lose consciousness, but it didn't seem I had a choice in the matter.

I woke back in bed with my bandages being taped.

"How much time has passed?" I demanded of the doctor, trying to sit up.

"Just a few hours, since we found you unconscious in your wardrobe," she easily pushed me back down. "You lost a lot of blood."

"Oh," I settled back again and gave her easy access to my side.

"There," she leaned back when she finished. "Do you think you could eat anything?"

"I'm not sure," I frowned.

"Well if you can't I may need to hook up your IV again," she stated.

"I'll try," I forced a smile as she nodded and left the room.

I had the oddest sensation to check under my bed for the man from the wardrobe. I stared hard at the dark corners of my room to make sure no shadows were moving. A secret part of me wanted him to be there. Waiting. He had confused me in the most fundamental ways and I couldn't even blame him for rupturing my stitches. That was all on me.

When I thought back on it, he'd only used defensive maneuvers with me. Nothing offensive. Why was that? It went against everything I knew. With his strength and my weakened state, he could have killed me easily if that had been his goal. I was ashamed to admit it.

A nurse returned with a tray of food that included a cup of tea. I reached for the tea first. The floral scent wafted toward me and my hand froze for just a moment before I picked it up.

"Can I have a water bottle too?" I asked. "I'm really thirsty."

"Of course," the nurse smiled and walked back down the hall toward the kitchen.

I set the tea aside and studied what was in front of me.

Things began to link together in my mind. I wasn't hungry, but I needed them to think I was eating. I hated waste, but it couldn't be avoided. I took half the sandwich from in front of me and slid it under the pillow next to me. A small unopened bag of veggie crisps sat on the tray as well. I pushed on it and saw that it was not losing air, so I opened it and ate some, then set them on my night stand.

The nurse returned shortly with the bottle of water.

"Here you are," he smiled at the half eaten plate and handed me the water.

I took the water and yawned hugely, acting like I was suddenly very tired.

"Thank you," I mumbled and holding the water close, I let my eyes close. I steadied my breathing and waited.

The nurse took the tray and left the room. I cracked open my eyes and when I saw that the room was empty again, I opened them fully.

Taking the water bottle, I tipped it and squeezed, ensuring that it had remained unopened and untampered with. Thankfully it had. I opened it and took a long pull. The cool water ran down my dry throat. I took the sandwich from under my pillow and threw it in the trash next to my bed as I sipped at the water. I placed the crisps under the pillow, just in case I didn't get another unopened bag of food any time soon.

I took stock of the events that had happened to me since I left work the Friday before my birthday. I'd jogged home and found a pre-emptive party in my house. I was dragged out to the Deflowering for Skyye at the HOPP, which happened to be closed before the explosion.

That couldn't have been a coincidence.

We ended up at a location of my choosing after the first location was closed, as I assumed it would fit the Defloweree's taste. That seemed to be a hit and she was well taken care of. Unless someone knew me very well, it was unlikely that my movements would have been tracked past leaving the first

HOPP.

When we left and something felt off I sent Skyye to her grandmother, then found Amadeus.

Too many questions unanswered there. Had he been trying to warn me about something? Then the explosion happened. Following procedure I reported to the scene, acted as first Dekka on scene, then left it in the hands of Dekka Marlon with the promise to copy her on my report.

I got home, wrote my report and... that's when things started to get hazy and my head began to ache. I swear I'd sent it and then gone to bed, but Dekka Marlon had assured me that she had not received my report.

I'd gone to bed and suddenly two days had passed and I woke up with a body swinging from the rafters. How could my mind be that blank. I rubbed the tattoo that had shown up one of the last times, but that could have just been an alcohol soaked weekend that I blacked out.

Jen. Who was Jen? I pushed that away. No need to further confuse details.

I'd sustained minor injuries that I couldn't remember this time. My body had been exhausted like I'd been awake and running for the entire forty-eight hours that was missing. My mind skittered away from the implication of some of the more intimate aches from the missing time.

I went to GrandIloquence and I was barred, somehow of my own doing, which I also didn't remember. My mother was vague and requested my presence at which point... again things were hazy.

I remember losing consciousness and my mother screaming something. I tried to bring the word into my mind, but it was like trying to squeeze hot sand in my palm. I let it go again.

Somehow, after passing out on my mother's doorstep, I'd ended up at my apartment where it had exploded as well, and I'd again been injured. This time severely. And yet, my skin was unburned and there were no shrapnel marks on my body.

My only injury seemed to be the gaping wound on my side, which managed to be nonfatal.

The fact that Dekka Marlon had seemed suspicious led me to believe that the Uniformity considered both explosions to be connected. With how few terrorist attacks there were, it made sense.

There was only one conclusion I could come to: either I was extremely lucky, or my mother had lied to me about where I'd been for the second explosion. Though I'd asked my mother why I lied to the Uniformity, I knew I would have had to lie about something and I knew my mother wouldn't lie to me unless it was important. I wasn't about to turn her over for any possible terrorist connection, because I had my own things to hide.

The trash bags. I needed to make sure they'd been destroyed.

I continued to lie in bed, thinking and staring at the ceiling as the sunlight began to creep into the room from the far window. The night had passed while I thought.

Whether my mother knew someone was drugging me or not, I could only think they were just trying to keep me from answering questions at the Uniformity.

I wondered again who the man was in my wardrobe. How had he gotten there? Why did he seem familiar? And how had he invoked the feelings he had with such a light pressure? It was as if he knew exactly how my body would react.

It wasn't something that I was ashamed of, but I did tend to have sex with men as a convenience, rather than women. I'd had a relationship with a woman in college and it hadn't been at all what I wanted. Coincidentally, the same weekend the tattoo had appeared, I'd also broken it off with her. She still hasn't forgiven me for it.

I let my thoughts run to Victoria for a moment, before letting them drift back.

So rather than starting a meaningless relationship, I took

my pleasure from the HOPPs when I needed it. Which honestly wasn't often, because I was always focused on my position within the Uniformity. This man, I know I'd never crossed paths with at a HOPP though his body seemed familiar.

Why hadn't I sounded the alarm? A random, Scourge-less male, shows up in my bedroom and my first reaction wasn't to tell everyone to track him down? How had the others known to find me so quickly? I'd distinctly heard running feet before I lost consciousness.

That led me to believe that he had told the staff that I'd been hurt. But that couldn't be true because that meant everyone knew he was here. I wish I'd seen his eyes. I could feel the laser blue of them now, and I wasn't even sure why I knew what color they were.

I'd never put myself first. It was always the job.

Why was that? I frowned. *Why was this the first I'd ever really thought about it? Or was it?*

I had some very vague memories of arguing with my mother over the state of the world when I was young. Then I'd hit puberty and something had changed. We'd watched documentaries on the way women had been treated before the Revolution. Rape had been an accepted everyday norm. Victims were blamed for their behavior, or their clothing choices, as the reason for such a horrible trauma befell them. Women hadn't been granted the right to vote until the first quarter of the twentieth century in a country called the United States of America. In many of those same states they hadn't been allowed to own property or hold positions of power until mid-way through the 19th century. In many other countries, even in the previous modern era, some women still were viewed as property. Arranged marriages to men five times their age. Sold and traded like livestock by their own family. Hiding in shapeless sack, they could still be raped and then killed by their own family to somehow disperse the shame that brought *them*.

Something in me had been horrified at the idea that it had happened to us first. That these lowly creatures had dominated us for thousands of years. The original societies of our cultures had been matriarchal, yet we'd somehow allowed men to take over. And why? Because they'd been physically stronger?

Because we'd let them.

There had been reasons that led to the fall of a matriarchal society, but they'd started with merely physical strength and women had kept themselves from fighting, which meant they couldn't, or rather, weren't allowed to defend themselves. It was all downhill from there.

In ancient Egyptian culture, women had been revered as gods because they could carry life. And only gods could create life. There were many accounts of female rulers during that time. Then it seems the culture began to crumble as men were allowed to lead, or as men inserted themselves into the picture. Like Antony and Cleopatra. A love that had decimated two cultures with war.

It was why, even without the promise of war like previous cultures, we were always trained and ready for a fight. It was why the Uniformity existed. I still took pride at the position I held.

I thought about the protein and vitamin packs I'd been taking since I hit puberty. Each person when they hit a certain point in their life was designed a perfect meal supplement and vitamins. It was also why many of us didn't get sick if we stuck to it. I suppose it wouldn't be hard to insert some kind of calming medication as well to keep the population pliable. It wasn't like Redacting, but the idea still made me deeply uncomfortable.

The sun was shining brightly when I heard footsteps approaching. I shut my eyes and evened my breathing.

The footsteps, two sets, stopped outside my room and paused. I recognized one as my mother.

"Is she alright?"

I almost started at the sound of *his* voice, but I managed to keep still.

"The nurse said she pulled most of her NuSkin," my mother huffed. "What were you thinking?"

"I go stir crazy in that room," he stated. "And I needed to make sure she was alright. She'd found a bag that triggered a memory and she started seizing. I came out to make sure she didn't hurt herself, then when the seizing stopped I put her in the shower to wake her."

Seizures?

"How is that possible?" My mother asked.

"She's been through a lot," his voice dropped as it began to sound miserable. "It's a miracle she hasn't already hemorrhaged."

"The Uniformity came yesterday and administered a memory download," my mother sounded exhausted. "They seemed satisfied with what they took and said that no charges were incoming, but..."

A memory download?! What about Ameudeus?!

"Yeah," the man nearly laughed. "But..."

They were silent for such a long time as I lay there that I nearly drifted off.

"I'm going to get some sleep," my mother broke the silence finally. "You should do the same, we've been up all night."

"I will," he said agreeably. "Soon."

"Goodnight, Daily."

"Goodnight," he responded.

Daily.

That had been the word my mother screamed. The sharp blue eyes flashed into my memory. In the crowd that Friday, walking away from the explosion site. He'd been at my mother's before the explosion at my own property too. Had he planted another explosion at my own property to cover something else up?

I heard a noise directly next to me and couldn't help

myself.

My eyes popped open and the man called Daily froze, then sighed. He'd pulled a chair next to the bed and was reaching for my hand. We stared at each other that way for what seemed like hours. When he started moving his hand toward mine again, I recoiled.

"I should have known you'd figure out the tea soon enough," he let his hand drop, defeated.

I continued to stare at him silently.

"How are you feeling?" He prodded as he settled back into the chair, as if preparing for a long chat.

"Like I got hit by a truck," I said honestly, studying him.

He nodded and continued to watch me. My head was pounding just looking at him.

"So your name's Daily?"

"Yes," he winced, then stared at me like he was expecting me to lunge at him.

"Who are you to my mother?" I narrowed my eyes and watched him as closely as he watched me.

"That's complicated," he looked away.

"Uncomplicate it," I told him. "We have time."

Daily lifted his arms and ran his hands down the front of his face while he breathed out. His eyes drifted to my tattoo and away.

"I can do one thing to help give you answers," he said behind his hands, then let them drop. "But it will only give you more questions, ones that I will happily answer but I won't be able to verify, as you won't remember."

"Remember?" I asked. "You mean you know about my time loss."

"Yes," he looked in my eyes. "Because it's my fault."

 "How could my memory issues possibly be your fault?" I scoffed.

"You need to watch this first," grimly, he dug in his pocket and handed me a mini drive.

I frowned as he placed the card in my outstretched palm, then stood to leave.

"Where are you going?" I wondered aloud as I studied the tiny card. "And what's on here?"

"I'm going to get some sleep," he said. "And you'll find out when you watch the videos."

"Videos?" I asked. "There are multiple?"

"Yes," was all he said before he left me alone.

I reached carefully for the drawer next to the bed. I knew there would be a small screen I could use to view the mini drive. Once I had the screen in my hands, I plugged the drive in, impatient for answers.

A file became accessible and I tapped on it to open, but it was password protected.

I frowned.

I tried a couple of my normal passwords with no luck. I looked around, but Daily had left so I didn't have him to tell me what it was. Then I got an idea, though it seemed unlikely. I typed it in and was shocked when it worked.

Jen.

Immediately, a video began to play and I was stunned to see my own face, though several years younger.

"Hello," the mirror image said. "I know you're confused."

"No shit," I said to myself.

"I know," the video said. "It's shocking, frustrating, and terrifying to not remember making this video."

I just gaped as the other me continued to speak. I seemed lucid, and completely aware of my surroundings, but I had absolutely no memory of making this video. Not even an inkling.

"To prove this is you, and this is not a drill I will reveal one thing that no one else knows, except you," she paused and took a deep breath. "Your diary of your most intimate secrets is on the bottom shelf of your bedroom bookshelf."

I paused the video and looked for some headphones, I didn't want anyone overhearing what she was about to say next. Once they were plugged into my ears and linked, I hit play again.

"When you were six, you cut out the inside of an old history book to hide it from obviously prying eyes. You also created a fake diary to fill with mundane things that looked exactly the same, so no one could tell the difference if you were writing in either, which you left as a decoy under your mattress. If you can, go to the bookshelf and look at that diary now. Page two-hundred-thirty-six will confirm this with your own handwriting."

I looked to the shelf across the room, then back to the screen.

"Before you go find the book," I continued on the screen. "There is something you need to know. And now that I know you have headphones in, I can say it."

I swallowed and looked directly at the camera.

"You have been an integral part of the Resistance since before you attended University."

"No," I shook my head. "That's not possible."

"It is possible and deep down, you know it," I seemed to answer myself. "You have been a sleeper for the movement for as long as you've been a part of the Uniformity. It's why you've experienced timeloss and why you were never compelled to report it, because you were afraid it was true."

I felt as if my entire world were crumbling around me. Everything I thought I knew was a lie. Everything I've ever done and achieved wasn't mine. My heart broke into a million pieces.

"There's something else," the me on the screen continued.

"What could be worse?" I shut my eyes.

"Daily is your lover."

"Nope," I opened my eyes and turned the screen off with that.

It was ridiculous. I would never take a man as a full time lover. It was social suicide to accept a man into a permanent part of your life. It would be like calling them an equal, which they were not. I shoved the screen into the side table and just stared at the ceiling.

I knew there was a way to confirm this, through my diary, but at the moment I didn't want it to be true. I wanted this all to be some terrible dream. Why would I risk everything I've built? How could I possibly have done this to my family?

My mother already knew. I squeezed my eyes shut as I realized that. Had she always known? But that didn't matter, because it wasn't true. Even if there was something in my diary, there was no way to truly verify the handwriting was mine. I could have written anything under-duress, but I would also have left myself clues.

How else did I explain the time loss? Redacting seemed the most plausible reason, which is why it had occurred to me before and I still didn't say anything to the Uniformity. Though, I'd also considered that they were the authors of the Redacting. How the Hades had the Resistance gotten the resources to produce a successful Redacting? It flew in the face of everything we knew to be true about what the Resistance was capable of.

Thirsty, I reached for the bottle of water next to the bed and drank deeply. The reason I was drinking the water led me to another question. Why has my mother been drugging me, or allowing me to be drugged? It seemed, if my apartment had been bombed that the Uniformity would then investigate my involvement in both attacks. It would have been standard to question such a coincidence. The fact that I'd been at both attack sites. Unless there were more? I'd have to ask.

If they did a download of my memories, then did they also have an account of my action after I woke up that first day? I suppose it might be easy to miss because I didn't focus on the body and all I really did there was clean. It's impossible to download an internal monologue, so they would have to rely on snapshots of that day. And if they were satisfied, did that mean they hadn't found anything? Or were they just waiting until I was healthy to arrest me?

If the Resistance were smart and wanted to protect me as an asset, then they would wipe my memory so that when I was questioned I would easily tell the truth and when my memories were examined they could be verified. The loss of memory would be easily explained if there was some sort of head trauma. But that could have been done with a physical attack on my person. So then what had gone wrong? Why hadn't I finished the mission and gone home? Why had I woken up where I wasn't supposed to be?

Unless the bombing was in conjunction with multiple attacks on any higher ranking Uniformity members.

My mind spun with the possibilities.

Soon the light began filtering in, shifted as early morning turned to midday. Food was brought, which I now considered suspicious. I didn't want to be drugged. I needed the truth. My mother did not come visit me as I expected her to, but if she assumed I was sleeping off my breakfast, it made sense.

It didn't take long after the breakfast tray was taken away that Daily poked his head in.

"Did you watch it all?" He asked me.

"No," I narrowed my eyes as he walked toward the chair he'd left next to my bed. "Why did you assume I didn't?"

"Because you never do," he shrugged and plopped into the chair. You usually get to about half way through the first video before stopping for a bit.

He smiled as if he knew exactly why I stopped. I narrowed my eyes. If he knew that, then he had probably watched most if not all the videos on here. He would know where my diary was, and it wouldn't be hard to forge an entry. So that meant I needed to take those with a grain of salt. And if I didn't normally finish the videos, then maybe I needed to push through them. There could be a hint hidden in them.

Lifting his legs, he reclined slightly so that his bare feet rested on the bed. He crossed them at the ankle and lifted his arms so that his head was hammocked by his hands. He closed his eyes and just sat there like that. Smug seemed to be coursing off him in waves.

Daily's dark hair curled just above the collar of his shirt, wet from a recent washing. His biceps bulged subtly under the short sleeves, and the front stretched over his chest, unable to hide the natural strength that rested there. I found my stomach pulling deep. I had the strangest urge to touch his chest and rest my head there.

I looked up to his eyes, which stared back at me with a blue as cold and sharp as ice from the bottom of a glacier. They were full of something that kindled a dark need. I felt the need to look away, so I forced myself to hold the contact. Though my body was reacting one way, my mind pulled away.

"The video," I cleared my throat and hummed to move past the sudden tightness in my chest.

"It said that I'm part of the resistance." I said quietly.

"Yes," he nodded. "You are."

"How is that possible?" I needed to know that not everything in my life was a lie.

"Because you questioned what you were taught," a fierce pride gleamed in his sharp eyes. "But they didn't like that."

"They?"

"The Uniformity," he said grimly. "You should really watch the rest of the video. Even after multiple times, you still do a better job of explaining it to yourself."

"You said that before," I latched onto the phrasing.

"What?" Daily looked back at me, as his gaze had shifted.

"Implying this isn't the first time I've watched the video."

"Because it's not," the shrug seemed awkward with the way his hands were behind his head. The elbows lifted as well as the shoulders and he looked away again.

"Get the book," I told him.

Immediately, he stood and walked to the bookshelf, understanding exactly what I'd meant.

Daily returned with a large historical text and handed it to me. I opened it to the middle and found my old diary. I hadn't really thought of it in years, or so I'd believed. I set the large volume aside and opened to page two-hundred-thirty-six in the small journal.

At first glance the writing was my own, though with a younger flourish I no longer possessed. Now, my handwriting was blunt, blocky, and to the point, rather than flowery, engorged by curves. That alone was an affirmation that it seemed like my writing. Anyone could have copied my handwriting now, but to track down an old style to lend credence toward the idea that I wrote this myself and long ago. That would take a great deal of patience and a large amount of gaslighting.

It was hard to think I was worth the amount of work it would take to create this lie. The Uniformity wouldn't waste resources like this. But then that only led to one possible conclusion.

I squeezed my eyes shut, before opening them and reading the words on the page.

Casandra,

This isn't a dream.

I have to be short, as you may not have much time to read this. The rest you will pick up on your own. I know you're observant and smart, because you're me. So here are the facts:

You joined the resistance on your 18th birthday.

Mom sent you to a Reconditioning camp, but you ran away.

You camped in the woods on your own and kept moving, knowing they would be looking for you.

You found Daily and he brought you to the Resistance, which was well hidden.

Together, you helped reform and arm the Resistance using your education and training.

You are the reason that they are as organized as they are.

When there was nothing more for you to do, you volunteered to be a sleeper and let yourself be ReDacted, first by the Resistance then again by the Uniformity.

Whenever there was a chance, Daily was your handler as well as your trigger. His presence is the reason you remember anything.

I made the video after the first time ReDaction failed.

I remembered everything and turned myself over to the Resistance for more ReDaction.

Daily always seems to be the key to your memory.

At this point, only he would know how many times you've been ReDacted and some memories may be permanently lost because of the frequency in which you had to reSubmit.

This is no one's fault except your own. You chose this because it is a worthy cause.

Accept it, move on and do what you must to dismantle the Uniformity.

Be Safe,
You

Finish the video.

I nearly laughed aloud. Evidently Daily knew me much better than I currently knew myself. It would be funny if it weren't absolutely enraging.

I couldn't argue with the facts because I couldn't verify them as yet.

The only thing I could do was watch the rest of the video.

I looked over and Daily was watching me intently. His casual, relaxed posture belayed the fire that burned blue in his eyes. The intensity of his gaze chilled me, but I did my best to make sure he had no idea. I kept his gaze, steady and stubborn.

Daily's face broke quickly into a grin that had me blinking in surprise. The moment was broken as he stood and turned to the door.

"Follow your own orders, Dekka," he called over his shoulder before he disappeared around the corner.

Of course he would know what was written in the book as well. My cheeks heated at the idea that he'd read the entire diary. There were some private details that I'd never shared with anyone. Secrets, guilty desires.

I shook myself as I looked at the tiny book. No where had I told myself to trust Daily. In fact, I'd made specific mention to trust my instincts.

The rest you will pick up on your own.

As if I was trying to tell myself something. Stating Daily was my lover in the video, knowing what my reaction would be and why I would stop watching the video then. Also knowing that Daily will have access to the videos and my diary meant I would need to imbed a message somewhere. So there was only one place to start, though my eyes were beginning to be heavy.

I pulled the small screen out of the side table to finish watching the video.

 The rest of the video was filled with unverifiable statements, similar to the diary.

There seemed to be a pattern to the cadence of my speech. I would drop out numbers occasionally, but there was an almost indistinguishable pause before some of them. I committed the number to memory, because I couldn't risk writing them down. When I was younger I would send secret messages to my sister, using a code book. A book we were both reading at the time. The first number would be a page number, the second would be the number of words into that page. So using that same technique, and assuming the diary was the book, I found the numbers I paused on in the videos. There were only four numbers.

Trust yourself.

That was the message. If anyone else had caught or knew how to crack my code, it would seem to be giving credence to the video. *Trust the video.* But in reality, it meant *Trust No One.* So my past self was definitely telling me I could not trust Daily. It also meant that I couldn't trust my mother. Even if she thought she was acting in my best interest, she may be operating without all the data.

On the off chance that this was an elaborate sting operation, I would continue to reserve judgment and see how the situation progressed. As of yet it appeared to be a black, writhing snake in the grass. If it was true that I'd had my memory triggered multiple times, what was the issue this time? Obviously something was different, as my mother was aware of my position within the Resistance, which it appeared she did not before. What I didn't understand was why she hadn't turned me in. It had taken less to send others away.

My mind scurried away from the awful memory. The angry, raised voices. The disappointment. It was becoming harder to push out the bad memories or the deep sense of deja vu that I'd been experiencing more and more often. Then something occurred to me.

"Daily," I called toward the hall.

I was surprised he didn't appear in the doorway immediately. With the way he showed up before, I assumed he was waiting right outside of the door. I shook off the uncomfortable idea that he was under my bed again.

He isn't the boogie man, for Goddess sake, I frowned at the door and forced myself to keep my eyes away from the floor.

"Daily," I called again.

When he poked his head around the corner I was startled, which had my frown deepening in displeasure. Why was I so affected by him?

"You rang?" He smiled and walked into the room, as if that was an old joke between us.

I stared at him coolly as he made his way to the chair and sat again.

"Why wasn't I Redacted again?" I wondered after he was settled.

"Ahh," his smile slipped sadly. "Well, mostly because if we mess with your brain again, it could mean you'd lose everything. There have been too many Redactions over the last few years."

"How is that possible," I asked. "I've never heard of anyone being Redacted so often that they were unable to withstand more. It was one of the reasons it was banned, because of its unlimited uses to brainwash people. The ability to steal and replace memories at a whim through neural triggering."

"You are proof that it isn't as *unlimited* as they led us to believe," regret flashed across his face. "They banned it because they knew the harm it could do, or rather, they banned it in theory rather than in practice."

"What does that mean?"

"This is the most frustrating part," Daily sighed and sat forward, rubbing his temples.

"I'm sorry my lack of memory due to the service I've

enacted for *your organization* is such a hassle for you," I ground out the words.

A seething anger was boiling beneath the surface. This was something I'd never felt before. As Daily looked back up, I saw a flash of something that had my stomach turning. It was gone just as quickly, but I recognized that look.

Rage.

"I'm sorry," Daily leaned back, holding his palms out. "You're right. I shouldn't be projecting."

There it was again; an apology. I stared at him suspiciously. If he was as angry as he let slip just a moment ago, why was he apologizing. He was able to hide the reaction quickly, but I wondered if he was used to just pushing my reset button when I questioned him.

"To answer your question," he continued while meeting my gaze. "I'm referring to ReConditioning."

"ReConditioning?" I clarified. "You mean the girls that are sent away for their unnatural urges?"

"Yes," Daily nodded. "It's a publicly used ReDaction program that no one talks about. Stripping these girls of memories that caused them to fall in love with a man, or wanting to submit to one, or wanting to help the Resistance."

"How is that possible?" I wondered. "Why isn't anyone fighting it?"

I pretended to be unaware of the practice, though I knew all about it. It was one of the few things I did not agree with the Uniformity on. They believed that submitting to men was so abhorrent, because it was what led to the near destruction of our planet. We are still cleaning up the mess.

"Because those that would, are fed a steady diet of pre-prepared food that is personally created for their taste consisting of all the vitamins, proteins, and complacency pharmaceuticals they can pump you full of," Daily said flatly.

"That can't be true," I shook my head and smiled, though I'd already had this thought earlier. "That sounds ridiculous, straight out of some science fiction nonsense."

"It's interesting," Daily stated.

"What is?"

"The way you'll easily assume betrayal from your own family, discontinuing your meals," he said. "But you have a hard time getting past the idea that a large unilateral entity such as the Uniformity, which controls the *entire* world, could possibly make things easier on themselves and ply their officers with mood stabilizers and soothers in order to get them to do their jobs without asking questions.

"You're having feelings now, aren't you?"

"What?" I feigned shock at the quick change in subject, this seemed to feed his ego. "Of course, I've always had feelings. This isn't new."

I let him continue with his explanation, though much of it was just confirming what I'd begun to suspect. Sweat dampened my palms as I considered the implications of what my paranoid mind had started to develop.

Sleeper Agent. Zombie Officer. Both sides had been playing me. It was time to figure out what I wanted.

"It's not new," he shook his head, as I redirected my attention to him. "But it's much more powerful."

I nodded as if accepting what he was saying without question.

"This is why we were drugging you," he frowned. "You've never had to come all the way out of your sleeper status. Before, you'd wake up, we'd have a few days together, then it was back to business as usual. But since we can't ReDact you, we had to pull you out."

"You're going to trust me to go back to work with everything I've learned?"

"I think you should rest," Daily got up suddenly.

"What?" I sputtered. "But I still have questions."

"Drink your tea," was all he said as he rounded the corner and out of sight.

I hurled my water bottle out of the doorway and yelled after him, but he didn't come back. My hands were shaking and my heart was pounding. Rage spewed from me and I felt helpless with it. I still had questions. I nearly got up, but the nurse was in soon after and pushed me back down into bed. A sharp prick in my arm had me gasping and glaring at the nurse, to which he responded with a cheeky grin.

I was not amused. I cursed, I yelled, I fought even though my side was on fire.

Then the light around his face dimmed and I couldn't be sure, but I think I told him where he could stick those needles next time before I lost consciousness.

When I woke, I was wearing a different night shirt and my linens smelled fresh. Groggily, I looked around. When I saw the duffel bag that had disappeared from my closet I remembered what I'd learned the last time I was awake. Then I realized there were several bags packed and ready.

"Good, you're awake," Daily smiled cheerily, though his smile didn't reach his eyes.

"You're leaving?" A quick panic in my chest surprised me. I looked down at my offending torso and glared, as if that would keep it from betraying me. It was beginning to be harder to control my emotions.

"We are," he grabbed two bags at a time and lugged them out the door.

I looked back at the doorway and began gently moving my legs to the side. When I found that they were stable and my side wasn't screaming in agony, I sat up and my feet touched the ground.

"Get dressed," Daily came back in and grabbed two more bags, then started to walk out again.

"Wait," I said and he paused at the doorway.

"We don't have much time," he said and continued out the door.

I considered ignoring his demand, but realized I wanted my clothes anyways. So why would I spite myself just to ignore his orders? I was just finishing up when he looked at me and smiled.

"I changed because I wanted to," I clarified. "Not because you told me to."

"Of course," he hefted the last two bags. "Follow me."

I crossed my arms and stared at him.

"Please?" He cocked his head to the side and struggled to contain the smile that pulled at the corner of his lips.

I rolled my eyes and relented.

"Where's my mother?" I asked as I walked out of the room for the first time in...

It was disconcerting how often I was unaware of the passage of time.

"Out," he stated as he walked with purpose toward the stairs closest to my room.

"And the staff?"

"Out too."

"All of them?" It was embarrassing that I struggled to keep pace with his easy walk.

"All of them," he confirmed.

"Why is that?"

"So when the Uniformity comes for you, no one will even know that you left, let alone where you were going, why, or who with," he threw over his shoulder. "It's unlikely with your mother's standing that she will be submitted to a memory search, but it's not impossible."

"Is she going to be ReDacted?" I asked.

"No," he shook his head as he started down the stairs, skipping every other one. "She was kept out of the loop on pretty much everything, and knew better than to ask questions. It's why she's been avoiding you and your questions."

I gritted my teeth and leaned heavily on the rail as I slowly descended the stairs.

"What does she think is happening?" I hissed out as I finally reached the bottom of the stairs, where Daily waited patiently for me. "What will happen if she does get a memory download?"

"As far as she knows, you're running away from the Uniformity with your lover so that you can live happily ever after," he grinned at what must have been a deep shock on my face, then turned on his heel and walked out the side door to the gardens. "So nothing will happen, except shame on the family name."

I huffed as I tried to follow quickly.

"But what about my memory issues?" I called after him.

"She knew better than to ask," he yelled over the howl as a heavy wind whipped around the lawn, pushing the grass down in odd shapes and shaking the hedge roses. "You can't download suspicions."

"The garbage bags," I remembered suddenly. "Did you find them?"

"You mean the bags full of evidence that would easily convict you of murder?" Daily laughed. "Yeah I found those in the boot of your car. I took care of them."

"Ok," I blew out a breath. "Did you know what happened?"

"It was an unfortunate miscalculation," was all he said.

I blinked as I exited the doorway and saw natural light. My eyes burned, but began to adjust quickly. I saw then that it wasn't wind, but a hovercopter.

My heart thudded into my throat as I nearly turned around and ran back inside. It had been a test after all and here was the 'copter to take me to ReConditioning. I shoved the panic down and observed, to the best of my ability, while holding the door open as a possible escape.

The familiar hedges, bushes and grass swayed wildly under the onslaught of the vehicle. The hovercopter had no propeller, despite the implication of its name. It was currently a grayish white as it matched the sky's cloud cover. If it weren't for the lush green of the perfectly trimmed grass and shrubbery, it would have blended in perfectly. The color could change in an instant, if the sky cleared. It only reflected what was above, not below. The vehicle wasn't normally used for transport, but Recon.

It ran on solar panels and the wind generated during flight, while projecting the sky to give itself direct cover while flying inconspicuously. It was silent, except for the wind force it created when close to the ground. Its shape was like a fat disk, built for incredible speeds. There were small wind tunnels on the underside of the craft that housed a large amount of small turbines, which helped create its perpetual motion. As long as it was moving, or there was sunshine, it charged its own battery. Unless it was being stored, it did not put down its landing gear. It was able to maintain perfect altitude while its engines ran, and the lift sat just a few inches from the ground. Barely a step up.

I couldn't see who piloted the vehicle as the windows were covered in two-way, matte solar panels that reflected the sky's color, like the rest of the craft. If you knew where to look you could spot the small lines that differentiated where the panels started and ended.

When they'd been invented they had been groundbreaking, as they could reflect an electromagnetic pulse instead of succumbing to it. Now they were standard issue to some branches of patrol in the Uniformity. Though not in large numbers.

Daily stood under the vehicle and beckoned me to follow. I looked back into the house and back at him. He could see my hesitation and just smiled, crossing his arms as if questioning my bravery. I growled internally before letting the door close and walking across the lawn. When I reached the small platform I stepped on, and it began to rise into the belly of the craft.

I wondered if I was allowing him to manipulate me, or if he was successfully manipulating me.

I nearly pitched over at the thought, but Daily steadied me as my balance faltered. I nodded my thanks and shook off his hold. I watched the view of my mother's estate fall away as we rose higher and higher. As it began to be cut off by the edges of the craft, I had an odd impulse to squat in order to see the estate for as long as possible. Instead, I stood very still and watched it disappear.

When the platform engaged with the craft and closed with a whistle of air pressure, I wondered if I'd ever see my home again.

The craft began to move faster as soon as the hatch hissed closed.

It felt like being in an elevator, with a barely discernible rise in acceleration. Though the vehicles were built for speed and could easily exceed mach two, there was generally no reason to reach those speeds unless traveling a long distance.

So imagine my surprise when Daily directed me to a chair with straps.

"We need to strap in," he gestured to a cushioned seat affixed to the wall.

He pulled it down and held the seat for me to sit. I gritted my teeth at the gesture, this time I would stand my ground. I crossed my arms and stared at him, a single eyebrow raised. When I did not immediately sit, he looked away from the straps he'd been untangling.

"I'm not a child," I told him. "I know how to sit and strap myself in."

"Ok," he shrugged good naturedly, though I thought I caught a hint of that rage again. He sat in his own seat, directly next to the one he'd chosen for me.

I looked around the small cylindrical room and found the seat opposite to his. I sat and strapped myself in, then met his eyes again. The sharp blue pierced into mine as he leaned over to the comm and pressed a button.

"Strapped," was the single word he said.

The sudden acceleration took me by surprise. I gripped my straps for support as it felt like I was being pressed deeply into the seat, before we finally leveled out. A small bag that hadn't been secured properly slipped its bindings and smacked me right in the forehead. I realized now why Daily had picked the other side.

I glared at his barking laughter.

"You did that on purpose," I threw the small case at him as his laughter continued.

"Serves you right," Daily shrugged. "You're the most stubborn woman I know, Cas."

The name reverberated in my head and it felt like my skull was splitting open.

CAS, *CAS*, cas, cas, *cas cas cas,* repeated over and over in my head. A different voice, different emotions. Something squeezed my heart so hard I could barely breathe.

"Shit, shit, shit," a concerned voice laid me down on the hard metal and I could feel my body convulsing.

A deep pressure surrounding my body seemed to still my shaking until it was just some slow and occasional twitching. My eyes returned to behind my lids and I tried to open them, but they felt stuck. It was like I couldn't quite open them because I couldn't move my eyes from above. I shook my head to right it, trying to wake myself up.

"Shh," the gentle voice soothed, I could tell it was Daily, but there was an echo of another voice that had said the exact same words to me. "Just lie still for a moment, you're safe."

I took the voice's suggestion as it suddenly seemed all I could do. I relaxed and ignored the heavy weight on top of me. My breathing evened and I was able to open my eyes. I looked into the sharp blue and realized that the comforting weight was the press of Daily's body. He'd covered me in a blanket, pillowed my head on his arm and rode out whatever the hell just happened.

"Why do you care so much?" My voice broke and I cleared it, pushing away the heavy emotion.

"That's a long story," he smiled sadly. "With any luck, you'll remember it on your own."

"Was that a seizure?" I asked.

"Yes," he slowly rose and helped me back into the chair.

I felt unbearably exhausted.

"Why did you hold me down?" I wondered. "I could have hurt you."

"Because I would rather be hurt than have you hurt by any number of objects in here," he gestured around the metal sphere, rife with edges that could easily do damage if I'd inadvertently struck any of them. The words he said struck a cord again, but it seemed off. Like someone else's voice in his mouth.

"Why didn't you just leave me strapped into the seat then?" I strapped myself in, and he did the same in the chair next to mine.

"For the same reason," he shrugged.

I let that one go, as the headrest was padded, and I didn't think I was in much danger being left strapped there. Though not being horizontal could have caused some neck issues. I brushed that away.

"Why did you call me Cas?" I asked.

"Did you remember anything?" His gaze narrowed and he waited for my answer.

"Not really," I reached up and rubbed my throbbing temple. "More like a feeling?"

An echo.

He waited as I gathered what scattered pieces I could.

"The name repeated in my head," I said. "I felt safe with the name, as if it were a term of endearment, or honor. Like I'd earned it."

"Yes," Daily sighed. "That's pretty close."

"Why do I have seizures when something triggers a memory?"

"We have a theory," Daily frowned and looked to the other side of the cylinder. "Do you know how ReDaction works?"

"Um..." I thought back to my years of training and the supplementary classes I took. "I vaguely recall that it was suppressing specific memories and replacing them with others, but it wasn't reliable and it was easily found through memory searches as the fake ones never matched completely."

"Broadly, yes," Daily nodded and rubbed his thighs. "Let's say we have a straight line to represent memory. It's filled with points representing important or formative memories. Following?"

I looked at him with a tired expression.

"Of course you are," he smiled apologetically. "Once upon a time you taught me this."

"I did?"

"Yes," he sighed before continuing. "So starting with point A as your earliest memory, we can categorize different points during that year with sub-dimensions: A1, A2, A3b, and so on. When we have an idea of how many memories a brain retains at any one time, it's easy to categorize them."

The information felt familiar but I couldn't see where it was going next.

"So, once specific memories are categorized, then you can create gateways."

"Gateways?" A small bell was ringing in my head, adding to the throbbing.

"Yes," using his thumb and forefinger on both hands he held them out and gestured with his left first. "Let's say, using your most recent experience as an example: this point is the point in your memory where you went home after the bombing of the HoPP and this other one is the point in which you woke the Monday after."

He pushed his right hand out second so that he was making a rectangle with his hands. I stared at his hands as if they would explain this faster.

"It's easiest to use two points that include sleep as the brain doesn't really remember sleeping."

"Ok..." I nodded to make him continue.

"So when taking a memory, it's also easiest to just," he pulled his hands together so that they touched. "Just tie it off."

"So you're not erasing and replacing?" I asked.

"Right," he nodded. "Just kind of, skipping over them. Then there's no red flags."

"Except the time lag," I reminded him.

"Right," he smiled and rubbed the back of his neck. "But it's undetectable. And any memory loss can always be accounted for as having too much fun, an injury, or losing track of time."

I thought of how often that happened to me and closed my eyes. My eyes burned. I'd been used for years and always questioned myself. Always wondered why I couldn't get a hold of my time losses. I'd nearly gone to a doctor more than once, but something had always stopped me. Some deep-seated doubt that maybe they would find me unfit for duty. I'd built a careful wall to keep people out, so they'd never see that I was broken. I had skipped making friends and going to parties because there'd been times where I'd woken up somewhere I hadn't gone to sleep at. I'd thought that maybe I'd just been overindulging.

My peers at University had assumed that I'd always been studying and was too stuck up to be around them. I'd missed out on so many experiences, so many relationships. And why? I still didn't know. All of my self-doubts and pressure to perform had all been because of the time loss. Who was I?

"Where are we going?" I whipped my head toward Daily.

"Uhh.." He jumped startled at my sudden intensity. "We are joining up with the Resistance."

"Good," I wasn't sure what I was going to do, but there would be a reckoning. "Was there really an explosion at my townhouse?"

"Yes," Daily stated.

"But I wasn't there was I?"

"No."

"How did I get this?" I pushed my hand between us and gently touched the long gash on my side.

"I removed your tracer," he smiled, slightly embarrassed.

"Tracer?" I narrowed my eyes and tried to see my side. "I never had a tracer. And this is way too big for a tracer extraction."

"They are standard issue with your final inoculations at graduation," Daily shrugged. "And I did the best I could. We couldn't call a doctor to do it, they'd probably leave the tracer in anyway. Plus it needed to look bad for them to believe you'd taken shrapnel. No sane person would injure themselves that badly on purpose."

"I didn't, and you think the Uniformity would put a tracer in me without consent?"

"I'm sure there was some small print somewhere with vague terms on a contract when joining the Uniformity."

"'Section 765; sub section e: While working under the guise of the Uniformity you will be periodically monitored and traced by various security items."

"Sounds about right," Daily grinned. "It must be frustrating being able to pull up an old contract, but not be able to remember yesterday."

"You have no idea," I squeezed my eyes shut and let my head loll forward, then something occurred to me. "Did you mark the tattoo?"

A cut had run through it after I'd woken up, like someone had been trying to cut it off my body.

"No!" The answer came too quickly. "It was cut in a fight we got ourselves into."

"Ok," I let the lie hang in the air between us. I didn't know why, but it felt personal as to why he cut at the tattoo.

Jen. Who was that? And why did he feel threatened by her?

I did my best to relax my body. I knew I wouldn't be able to sleep, but I should be able to rest. I'd done so in worse circumstances.

Daily left me alone to my thoughts and stayed blessedly silent.

I kept my eyes shut and let my mind wander. In my mind it had only been a few days since all of these unbelievable events occurred. I was on the edge of accepting it all as true. How else could I explain all of it? This was beyond the scope of anything I'd ever heard of the Uniformity doing. If this was an elaborate ploy to expose me as a Resistance Sympathiser, what would they have to gain? Nothing. If anything, they would have lost an asset with a witch hunt. So who had the most to gain? The Resistance.

By using elaborate gaslighting techniques, they could have tricked me early on. I could have been forced to give that video message, leave the writing in my journal. It would explain the sporadic missing time and the fact that I had no memory of anything to corroborate what had been established as supposed fact.

Silence reigned until there was a light static from the comm across the hatch. Daily unstrapped and walked over to answer. A quiet and muted conversation transpired and then he walked carefully back to the seat next to mine. I didn't move, hoping he thought I was sleeping and would continue to be quiet.

"We'll be there soon," he said softly.

Of course he knew I was awake. I wondered idly how they recruited Daily. The fact that he hadn't been affected by The Scourge meant that men could grow up outside the small communities where most of them lived and still be unaffected. Perhaps it had been a sufficient amount of time that men could live beyond their small walls.

Something struck me about the idea that it was safe for men outside the communities they'd been forced to stay in. Why weren't there more then? Unaffected men were still an extremely rare sight. And I still saw boy children affected by The Scourge. If it was safe, what prompted the deformities still? Perhaps it was inherent in carrier women. I chewed on that for a while.

"Where did you grow up?" I startled him with my quiet and pointed question.

Daily seemed to have been deep in his own musings, he narrowed his eyes.

"Not in an Amish, Quaker, or Dutch Community if that's what you're asking."

"How did you know that was my intent?"

"You have several steps of acceptance when you're

working to regain your memories," Daily told me matter of factly. "This is one of them."

"What steps?" I demanded.

"Similar to the steps of grief," Daily gave me a crooked grin and counted on his fingers. "There's Confusion, Anger, Fighting, Questioning: Yourself, the Uniformity, the Resistance, Gaslighting Assumptions..."

I was very uncomfortable how accurate this list was.

"And of course my favorite, acceptance."

"Why is acceptance your favorite?" I wanted to know.

"Because you kiss me," the goofy look he beamed at me could only be genuine.

"You wish," I frowned.

"Nah," he lifted his shoulders and let them fall. "I just miss you. The fact that this will be the last time we have to go through this is exciting. We can finally start our lives together. We've had a lot of beginnings, even some endings, but never a middle."

I stared at him as he babbled excitedly, like a child.

"How do you know I won't just immediately leave you when I remember everything?" I asked him. "What if I met someone else and they are just as important to me?"

"You haven't," Daily forced a smile that made my stomach turn. "I would know."

"I don't know," I shrugged and sent him a look of pity. "You see, I'm finding out that I have a lot of secrets recently. Did you ever think that maybe I've kept things from you once I've remembered who you are? Are you telling me we've never lied to each other? Not once?"

I could see I'd hit a nerve as Daily looked away, before looking back with a smile that once again didn't quite reach his eyes.

"You don't know us yet," he told me simply and firmly. "But you will. And you'll kiss me."

I was confused by the panicked tightness in my chest at his surety. He had an amazing amount of faith in our purported relationship. I wondered what he would look like when I disappointed him, as I was sure to. If this was really the last time I would be gaining back my memories, then I wouldn't need to pretend to like him anymore. There was no way I could live up to this Guinevere and Arthur scenario.

I looked away when my throat seemed to close and I swallowed convulsively. Closing my eyes, I let myself relax again for the rest of the trip.

We landed with a thump as the storage gear descended. Daily was quick to unstrap and offer a hand, which I ignored.

I unstrapped myself and looked up at the swish and slide of the flight deck opening and a figure descending the flat ladder built into the wall. I was curious, so I stared at them as they moved downward.

Something seemed familiar about the way the person moved. Confident, almost challenging, which continued as they stopped at the bottom and turned. Catching my gaze they returned it, cocking their head and raising a light colored brow over the top of dark flight glasses. I couldn't ascertain a gender from their clothes, as they were of an androgynous fit. Olive colored baggy fatigues. Head was shaved, which did not help either with my determination.

"Ready?" Daily addressed the pilot who nodded toward him and walked onto the round platform in the middle.

When we'd both followed suit, the pilot pulled a lever for the manual hatch drop. The sound of pressurization was the only indication that it had opened and without the sound of the air moving the surrounding flora, it was hard to imagine we'd been in a hovercopter at all. Light greeted the opening. I blinked as my eyes readjusted to natural light again. I could see a host of evergreen trees surrounding the clearing we had set down in. This confused me because evergreen trees in this large amount were located all the way on the other side of the continent. A large number of trees had been destroyed where I lived during the initial in-fighting happening when the countries were trying to figure out how to govern and form the current Uniformity.

Silently, the hydraulics lowered us to the ground where we were immediately overrun by copies of the pilot, holding rifles and all other manner of weaponry on our position. The only thing they were missing were the large shades covering their eyes. Even seeing all of their eyes, I was just as lost in trying to determine their genders. They all seemed to ooze out of the trees almost as silently as the platform's descent had been.

The pilot made a few hand gestures, which had the soldiers relaxing and saluting.

One soldier stepped front and center, then using quick hand gestures foreign to me, they conveyed a message to the pilot who nodded and gestured Daily and myself forward.

"Follow me," Daily grinned and waved at or acknowledged everyone we passed. Most did their best to remain passive masks, but there were a few that cracked. They were happy to have him back.

With me, however, there seemed to be a mixed reception. While facial expressions stayed placid, body language was always a tell. If I was the hero I was purported to be, then why were some of these soldiers not only nervous, but a few were outright hostile.

One specific person never let go of their weapon, but instead of aiming it at me they had it at the ready, pointed downward. It was a position I often taught my recruits, for use if you were in hostile territory and were unsure if you were about to walk into a room of armed terrorists or drooling toddlers. Their eyes burned into mine as I walked past them and began walking a tight decline. Dirt and rocks crunched under my boots. Eyes the color of whiskey that seemed to shift with light and movement. Expressive enough that I could see a dry hatred there, but I was confused about what I'd done to them. Wasn't I the one that suffered for this?

They reminded me oddly of my mother's eyes, but I pushed that away. There was only one person other than my mother that had those eyes, and she was dead. I nearly stumbled as a wayward branch reached out and grabbed my ankle.

The reminder cut deeply and I looked away, walking as confidently and calmly as possible. As if I was not walking into a viper's nest. Though if it turned out to be a den of snakes, they were about to find a Sidewinder in their midst.

The corner of my lips curved upward as I prepared myself for a challenge. I had the oddest urge to giggle. My head felt light and a twinge in my side reminded me I was not at full strength, but I didn't care. I would do what was necessary if I had to. A faintness nearly had me stumbling, but I caught myself. I was shaking lightly, but I just chalked that up to adrenaline. I did my best to continue to follow Daily, but my legs began to feel sluggish. I blinked as the light around me seemed to dim.

"Where's the sun?" I asked.

Daily turned with a look of confusion on his face, which quickly turned to panic.

"Medic!" He yelled, and rushed toward me as the ground seemed to rise up to meet me very quickly.

I tried to push at Daily and tell him that I didn't need or want his help, but I don't think he could hear me over his own shouting. He lifted the side of my shirt and I glared, attempting to push it back down. My hand was slapped away.

"Goddess, what a hack job," a churlish voice reached my ears as my sight continued to fade. "Remind me to never let you near patients, or anything medical related again."

"It had to be done," Daily insisted.

"You had one job," the voice rose angrily. "Get her here in one piece."

"She's in one piece," Daily defended.

"Barely," the voice was very close, near my ear. "It seems like you were determined to cleave her in two. You nicked an artery at some point, it's been slowly bleeding into her abdomen for days."

"What?" Daily seemed to try and look, but he was slapped away. I tried to laugh at the turn of events but I just coughed up something wet.

"We need to get her on a table," the voice sounded farther and farther away. "NOW!"

There seemed to be a flurry of movement and suddenly I

was floating. I looked up and marveled at the blue of the sky. Crisp. Just like Daily's eyes. Every time I closed my eyes, someone shook me and told me not to sleep.

But I was so tired. And I didn't really want to fight anymore. I felt warm and I was floating, so I let myself drift.

I woke an unknowable time later. Machines beeped and whirred around me. I tried to take a deep breath but I started choking on something. When I attempted to use my hands to pull at it, I realized I was tied down.

The machines began to beep faster and something like a siren wailed. Soon after, one of the genderless soldiers came in smiling and tried to gesture for me to calm down. With their hands they mimed pulling something out of my throat.

I nodded my consent as much as I could.

The soldier nodded in response and gripped the bottom of my jaw with one hand and with the other gripped the tube attached to my mouth. I tried to relax but I wanted to vomit at the feeling of something sliding back up my throat. When it was out I gasped a breath and wretched. I coughed and dry heaved for a time. My hands were freed then a glass of water was pushed into them. I gulped the cool liquid down, then immediately threw it up again into a waiting container.

I tried the water again, this time sipping slowly, which seemed to have a much better result as it did not immediately come back up. My throat burned as if it were an open sore. Slowly I became aware of someone rubbing my back as I leaned over the side of my bed, ready to heave again.

Weakly, I looked over my shoulder and met Daily's sharp blue eyes. Face unshaven with several days worth of growth, his eyes were shadowed and dark.

"This.-" I coughed.

"Yes?" Daily seemed intent on my every word. Good.

"-is your fault," I croaked.

He bust out laughing and I stared at the sight. The easy mirth of the relieved. When he was finished, he wiped his eyes and looked at me again, this time a bit regretfully.

"Yes," he sobered. "It is. But I would do it again as long as I get to keep you this time."

"I'm not a possession to keep," I responded hoarsely, unnerved by the implication.

"Oh, I know," he chuckled lightly. "Trust me, you've proven that time and time again."

"Why do you want me?" The sudden query took me as much by surprise as it did him.

"Well," he hissed air through clenched teeth and scrubbed a hand through his hair. "That's a loaded question."

"Forget it," I brushed the thought away with my hand. "I'm not in my right mind."

"Hey, now," Daily pushed me back down as I tried to get up. "Just calm down and be patient. I know that's hard for someone as stubborn as you."

I pushed back and had zero pain in doing so, if a little weakness. It surprised me enough that I let him push me back the next time, so I could lift up my tree green hospital gown. When I pulled it aside, I gaped. The wound was not only healed, there was barely a scar. As if it had been years. My heart dropped as I turned back to Daily.

"How long?" I demanded.

"Only a week," he put up his hands in a peaceful gesture.

"How is that possible?" I demanded, gesturing to my side. "Not even the best doctors in the Uniformity can do this."

"They can," an annoyed voice from the doorway drifted in. He walked in, the tone mirroring his demeanor.

My stomach did a flip flop. His head wasn't shaved like the others. He wore a green lab coat over his fatigues, I could tell he was a man. He was also untouched by The Scourge and tall because of it.

"They just don't," he scribbled on a clipboard, which he set at the end of my bed and took out a pen light from his breast pocket. "Follow the light please."

I did as he asked and blinked repeatedly when it turned

off.

"Good," he put the pen light away and scribbled on his clipboard again.

His hair was just a bit longer than many of the soldiers I'd seen, straight and messy with it. His jaw was square and his eyes flashed a liquid green I'd never seen before. Something like a piece of glass I'd picked up off a beach once, a shard of a broken bottle. While I studied the doctor I could feel Daily's eyes on me. I wasn't sure why, but I looked away from the doctor.

"What do you mean, 'they don't'," I asked.

"Just what I said," his voice was impatient and annoyed. "You're lucky to be alive Casey."

"How do you know my name?" I waved off the question before it could be answered. "Nevermind. I'm sure we met in the past I don't currently remember."

"Still no memories?" He qualified, this time to Daily. "This is the longest she's been around you without remembering the majority of it. Is there anything she would be repressing?"

"Of course not," Daily sounded offended. "I would never do anything to jeopardize the mission or her."

"Didn't mean you," the doctor mumbled while he scribbled more notes. "I'll be back to check on you later. I would say more than likely you're ready to get out of that bed. I just want to monitor you for the next twenty-four."

I watched him as he avoided making eye contact with me, then left the room without saying anything further. I stared at the dark brown wood paneling of the room. It matched the same in the hallway and on the ceilings. The floor was a surgical white vinyl tile that would be easy to clean and sanitize. There were no windows, so I had no idea what time of day it was. The fluorescents were burning my eyes as they suddenly felt very dry.

"That was Jensen," Daily explained lamely. "He's our medical doctor."

Jen. The name swirled in my head. Was it a coincidence?

"But men aren't allowed to become doctors," I corrected.

"Well he's as close as we've got," Daily shrugged.

"Ok," I laid back on the bed and closed my eyes. "You can go now."

"I'm not leaving you," Daily challenged.

"Look," I turned my head to meet his sharp gaze. "Thank you for everything you've done, as I'm sure you think it was all in my best interest, but I have no idea who you are. And right now, I just want some peace and quiet. And before you suggest it, no you can't just sit there quietly. Please just go."

For a moment Daily sat there and I wondered if he would leave. His gaze was hooded, as if he were wrestling with something he didn't want me to see. Then his eyes softened as he looked into mine. It made me wonder what he saw there. He nodded curtly and left the room.

I sighed in relief. I think he meant well, but his presence was beginning to suffocate me. The constant optimism that had... something else. So sure that I would remember him and everything would go back to normal... for him. I wasn't even sure that I wanted to remember. I let my eyes close and let thoughts just drift through my mind.

Relaxed, I could smell the water and feel the dappled sunlight on my skin. There were small distant splashes from the secret lake I'd found full of fish no one knew about.

Even with my eyes closed I could feel the evergreen trees shifting around me. I became one with them and touched the rock beneath me. It's cold, rough ridges bit into my palm. I took a deep breath of fresh air and exhaled slowly.

I'd been at the ReConditioning camp for several weeks now. They had tagged my case as low priority - low-grade fantasies, so I hadn't needed to be subjected to the shock therapy they tended to prescribe for those who were wholly perverse.

It was my sixteenth birthday today.

I wondered what my mother was doing. If she was eating a piece of cake in my honor. I hoped she choked on it.

I was angry with her for sending me here. No amount of begging had changed her mind. I'd railed. I'd thrown things. But I'd still been packed off to the middle of nowhere. The wilderness that surrounded the camp deterred a great many girls from attempting to leave, but not me. I was always back by lights out, so they didn't really care much about what I did during the day.

I had a few weeks left before they could send me home. After just two conversations with a counselor they could tell I didn't need to be here, and yet here I stayed. Because the Camps were beginning to lose their funding, and I was from a rich family. Basically, they couldn't afford to send me back.

Instead they gave me pretty much anything I wanted, including free reign of the facilities. Once they realized I was an avid hiker they'd given me a map, compass, and some basic hiking supplies. I'd considered taking them and just hiking out, but they only ever gave me a half days worth of supplies. Looking at the map, we were in the mountainous area of Damocles Blade. Once it had been called the Rocky Mountains, but some higher up had thought to rename it something more romantic after the Uniformity took over.

It would take several days to hike out, or get anywhere near civilization without a vehicle.

I cursed my mother again. Damn her for allowing this.

If I hadn't been caught by one of her prudish friends, this wouldn't have happened. I dug my fingers into the side of the rock until it became too sharp, then relented. My anger surged with teeth made of iron, gnawing on my belly.

The servant had more than likely been transferred. I was annoyed that I couldn't remember his name, and his face was already fading. There would be another. They were all just play-things anyway. To be used and discarded at whim.

Just because I'd let him top me, *once*, and that harpy from the board my mother served on walked in.

I could take some of the blame - that I'd tried to instigate something in the kitchen, and had been giggling at the ridiculousness. The boy had looked just terrified by the idea of someone walking in. I say "boy", but he'd been a bit taller than me, lanky and a few years my senior. I'd taken great pleasure in his fear. But then someone did walk in, and it hadn't been my mother or the staff.

Why had my mother chosen to give a tour that day? My brows knit together in frustration.

Her spinelessness had cost me training time at school. That could also cost me a place at University. There'd be hell to pay if that happened.

So I hiked, and I tried to shake off this aggression. I couldn't spar with anyone, but at least I could explore. On my second day of hiking I'd found a tiny creek that wasn't on the map. Finding it odd I followed it back to its source, which also wasn't on the map. And that had been how I'd found this nice sized lake, complete with a waterfall. There had been some recent ice melts that had caused the small reservoir to overflow. Otherwise, it normally drained into an underground river that seemed to connect farther down the mountain inconspicuously. Walking around the bank, I'd found the logs and debris that had caused the lack of flow into the dark underground cavern.

I made a job of clearing the debris so the flow was no longer constricted. That immediately ended the little creek I'd found.

It had only taken a week for it to dry and become nearly indistinguishable in the surrounding landscape. Eventually the creek would have dried on its own, so it was luck for me that I'd happened on it myself. And now I had my very own secret lake.

I'd come here every day since then, unless the weather had caused the counselor to ban outdoor activity for that day. I stretched and rolled my neck. The light was beginning to fade, and the shadows around me were getting longer. I knew it was nearly time to leave.

A splash, larger than the fish I was used to, broke the near silence of the woods.

I blinked my eyes open and kept very still.

Suddenly, I was no longer alone. A body was cutting across the little lake with fast, smooth strokes.

A wave of irritation that someone else had found the lake nearly had me standing up and shouting at them. Who were they to ruin my secret place?

Before I could, he stood at the edge of the lake, his back to me. And the body was that of a boy, or rather, a man. He was not lanky, but he was tall. He stretched and the muscles of his naked back and shoulder rippled. The light danced off of him as it hit the rivulets of water.

I wanted to shake myself. He glowed in a way that could have only been ethereal. I must be hypothermic. It was warm, but not warm enough for heat stroke. Dehydrated. I must be dehydrated.

I reached for my canteen while I kept him in my sights, afraid he would disappear before I could confirm if this was real. I'd never seen muscles like that before.

I was so distracted that I knocked the canteen over, and it hit directly on a rock below, causing a crack to stun the silence.

The man whipped around and looked right at me. We stayed like that for a while before he turned and, naked, walked into the woods.

I held my breath for a time before letting it out. If it weren't for the lingering ripples of water crossing the lake, I would still question whether or not he even existed.

I awoke panting.

What in Hades? I felt like that might just be my new catch phrase.

The machine's beeps and whirs continued monotonously, except for the heart monitor, which sounded erratic. I calmed my breathing in an attempt to get it under control.

The room was as empty as when I'd fallen asleep, dark paneling and all. Daily hadn't tried to sneak back in after he left. With no one to stop me, I threw my legs over the bed and stood. I did this slowly to make sure I wasn't pushing myself too much and making things worse than they already were.

My legs held and I moved my arms so that I was standing on my own. I tested the range of motion in my arms and leaned from side to side to see if anything hurt. Nothing did. I still felt a little weak, but that wasn't an issue. Doing a few squats, I tested my legs as well. Everything seemed to be functioning properly.

I found a set of basic overlarge fatigues folded on the chair that Daily had occupied. I took this as permission to go about my business and slipped into them. I also found a hair tie to pull back my knotted hair. I made a mental note to track down a brush, though remembering all the skinheads I wondered if I would be able to.

I put on my trusty boots and looked around hopefully for a weapon. No such luck. I walked out of the room and found two corridors. One left and one right. Without hesitating I picked a direction at random and began walking, careful to note where I was going.

I walked until I heard voices raised in argument. It was the first time I'd heard more than one voice at a time since I arrived, as everyone seemed to be using hand signals rather than speech. But that hadn't stopped Daily from speaking, or the doctor they called Jensen. I could hear his voice above the others, asking for calm before they all quieted again.

Rather than enter the room, I stayed outside to listen while they were unaware.

"Cas has been through a lot," Jensen sounded tired and some part of me wanted to comfort him.

I shook away the feeling. Where had that come from? My head throbbed lightly at the use of that name again.

"I know some of you are very excited to meet her, or even reintroduce yourselves to her, as that may be," there was a small cheer from a few of the soldiers. "But you all need to understand the threat still exists for us, and for her."

"Anything could set her off," Daily's voice chimed in. "The sound of a once familiar voice can trigger a memory, which normally would be alright, but something is blocking it. To the point where she seizes when she remembers nearly anything."

"She was kept sedated for a while under the Uniformity's nose, but she will quickly become a target and they will search for her," continued Jensen, as if Daily had not spoken. "So we need to batten down the hatches. No wandering the Edge."

There was a chorus of outraged shouts.

"What are we supposed to do for fun?" Demanded one.

"Are we prisoners now?" Asked another.

"Until we know the threat of exposure has been tamped down, we need everyone to stay close," Jensen pushed through the shouts.

"We are at a critical juncture," a new voice joined Jensen's and the entire room went silent, as if someone flipped a switch. "We can not, under any circumstances, be exposed now. Everything that we have worked for will be for nothing, and it will be life as a slave all over again."

The voice sounded feminine but it was hard to tell. I crept a bit closer to listen. It was strong and sure.

"Anyone who has a problem with that can talk to me," there was silence followed by the soft click of a door closing.

"The Organizer is right," Jensen told the room. "You can be happy about the circumstances, or you can dig ditches for a while. Your choice."

I stood as his voice sounded like it was coming toward me. Jensen stopped at the doorway as soon as he saw me, his brows suddenly knit together. He stepped forward while grabbing his pen light, then flashed it quickly between my eyes. Satisfied with what he saw, he replaced the light and continued walking.

"Mess is this way," he called over his shoulder.

I looked into the room, full of now arguing subordinates, and saw Daily trying to explain something with lots of big hand gestures to a few of them. I turned to follow Jensen, trotting to catch up with him.

"What did you remember?" Jensen asked me as I caught up to him.

"I remembered being in the ReConditioning Camp," I told him.

"Are you in pain?" Jensen continued, without stopping.

"No," I stated, huffing a bit to keep up. "Surprisingly."

"Good," he seemed to increase his speed just enough that I couldn't walk side by side with him or look at his face.

I paid attention to the turns we took in order to get to the mess hall.

"A cabin has been prepared for you."

"A cabin?" I asked.

"Yes," with a curt nod he gestured to the door ahead of us. "Here's the mess. I've got things to do."

With that, he turned and left. I wondered why he wouldn't look at me, or why he didn't want to talk to me. His shoulders hunched had been hunched with thinly veiled hostility. I had no idea what I'd done to cause such anger. Shrugging it off, I pushed the door open and walked into the mess.

It was empty, as the rest of the crew seemed to be in the meeting hall. That was a relief as I wasn't excited by the prospect of people who knew me, by reputation or experience, without some knowledge of their existence.

Seeing the food lined up, my stomach growled painfully. It was nothing special, oatmeal. But there were bananas as well, which surprised and pleased me. I grabbed the hot cereal and a banana, then looked around for a place to sit. That was when I heard the sounds of people coming down the hall that I'd just entered from.

My eyes flew around the room and I saw another exit. I moved quickly through it as a large number of people seemed to infest the area I'd just been in. I let the door close softly behind me as I realized I'd gone through an exterior door. The bright, crisp light of morning poured onto my skin from above the set of concrete stairs. I walked up them slowly and emerged in a canopy-covered clearing.

The canopy was made of a holed material the same color as the trees. Under it were parked vehicles, munitions, and a gaggle of soldiers either at post or milling about. I looked around, suddenly uneasy. Was I supposed to be out here? No one had stopped me.

I looked around and saw a bench made from a fallen log in a large patch of sun. Gravel crunched under my feet as I made my way over to it. I sat and sighed as the sunlight played over my skin in the cool morning air.

I peeled my banana and took a small sweet bite before breaking up the rest to put in my cooling cereal. I set the peel next to me as I took the first bite. It had been a long while since I'd had a banana. Especially in oatmeal. I savored it as I ate the small bowl of food.

"Enjoying the banana?" Daily's voice drifted over from the top of the stairs.

Hands in his pockets he made his way over to my seat, then, taking the banana peel in hand, he sat. I continued to eat, trying to salvage the small amount of peace I'd felt just a moment ago.

"I made sure that there were some available," he continued as if I'd answered. "I know how much you love them."

I swallowed and set the half full bowl aside. It suddenly did not seem as appetizing. Like the peace I'd felt, my hunger melted away as my stomach turned. I looked into his sharp blue eyes.

"Why did you blow up the HoPP?" I asked him.

"Orders," Daily shrugged. "It was a statement that had to be made."

"Even if there were casualties?"

"I'd evacuated the place," Daily crossed his arms. "I did my best to minimize any and all loss of life."

"When you approach a familiar target, one you've been

around before," I asked. "How do you approach it?"

"With caution," Daily's eyes narrowed. "What are you trying to say?"

"Trying to get you to understand something," I told him. "What else do you do?"

"Keep your guard up and approach the situation as if you did not know them," he continued. "For in essence, you may not, depending on the amount of time that has passed. They could be an entirely... new... person..."

Daily's voice trailed off as I watched it dawn on him.

"You're saying I'm being too familiar," he stated.

"Yes."

"And you want me to approach you as if I don't know you?" Daily clarified.

"Yes."

"I'm not sure that I can do that," Daily seemed hurt.

"This is what you need to understand," I blew out a breath before turning to face him. "I don't care."

His mouth opened as I let my filter fall off.

"Right now, at this moment, I have no idea who the hell you are. I don't care about you, I don't care about the Resistance. I have this constant feeling of deja vu that I can't shake, and it's not helping me remember anything. And you sitting here telling me about myself doesn't help either," I put up my hands, as it seemed he was going to try and hug me and I did not want to be touched. The feelings I'd been holding back came spewing out of my mouth. I stood to emphasize my need for space and moved in front of him as I continued. There was no need for a farce anymore. "In fact, it's creepy as Hades."

Wounded, he looked away, but I had an overpowering impulse to push on. To hurt him.

"I don't know you. I don't want you to touch me. New rules, starting now," I put my hands behind my back to communicate how much I did not want to be touched as he sat, looking away from me. I moved over and pushed back into his view, so I knew he was listening to me.

"Stop seeking me out. Stop talking like we know each other. Stop making goofy eyes at me. I don't know who you are. Period. If I want to see you, I will find you. If you think about me, push me out of your head. Stop looking at me like I'm being super predictable and you think it's cute, because it's not. It's horrifying, terrifying, and fills me with an anger I can't even begin to explain to you."

Daily nodded weakly and this time I let his eyes drift away, but I drove it home one last time.

"So just *stop*. Pretend like you don't know me, because I sure as Hades don't know you."

I turned, and walked away. I needed to find some peace and work off this anger. I couldn't let the hurt on Daily's face affect me. He needed to realize that his pushing wasn't welcome. As I headed off into the woods I saw Jensen entering a room off the side of the building he'd been standing in front of. I could have imagined it, but I thought he'd looked smug.

Had he heard the exchange? I hadn't exactly been quiet about it. There were a few heads that turned as I passed them. I'm sure it was a hell of a scene, but at the moment I didn't care. I just needed to find some quiet so I could be alone with the mess of my mind. It was becoming hard to think.

Following my instincts again, I walked up a slight ridge and found the makeshift hangar where we'd landed. All of the equipment was parked, locked and protected with the same material that covered the base down below. No wonder the Uniformity hadn't found them.

They were doing a good job of staying hidden.

I walked across the small clearing, nodding to a few sentries that stood watching. They eyed each other, as if not sure how to address me, so they just kept still. Sometimes no greeting was better than the wrong one.

I ignored them, as they did me, and continued into the cover of trees. I memorized my surroundings as I moved so it would be easy enough to make my way back, if that's what I even wanted.

I followed the deep feeling of familiarity and found my way to the small lake. I remembered hearing somewhere that ReConditioning Camp had been closed due to lack of attendance, at least the one located here. So the fact that the lake was overflowing with water again wouldn't matter. The camp being so close to the Resistance base couldn't be a coincidence.

I made my way around the lake's edge and found the rock I'd been meditating on in my new memory. As soon as I touched it a profound sense of calm engulfed me and my mind quieted. It was as if my body recognized the place more thoroughly than I did. I sat down and pulled my legs up. The muscle memory this rock triggered was painful and pleasant at the same time. Like a tendon I had forgotten to stretch for a long time.

I closed my eyes and breathed in the scents around me, letting the sunlight play on my skin, like I did in my memory. The sound of the waterfall was soothing in a way I hadn't realized I'd needed. After a while I could hear the small splashes of fish as their habitat returned to the quiet movements of the forest.

From my stomach, something pulled me off the rock. I suddenly had the very real need to be floating, weightless. I stripped and stepped into the cool water. It wasn't frigid, but it was cold and I shivered with it as I stepped in deeper. The water was clear and I could see my feet as I moved, until I kicked up the sand and dirt.

My stomach clenched as the water reached my midriff. Before I could change my mind I dove in, submerging myself in the chill. Then I rolled onto my back and let myself rise to the surface. The warm sunlight was a welcome change as my body adjusted to the temperature of the lake. I let my eyes close and let my mind drift as I did.

Normally I would never let my guard be down, but there

was something about this place that made me feel secure and safe, as I'd never felt anywhere else. Besides, no one from the Resistance would challenge me if their orders were anything to take seriously. If someone from the Uniformity happened upon this location, which was entirely unlikely, then they would ask questions first before shooting a naked, unarmed woman in the middle of the tiny lake.

On top of that, it would be impossible to sneak up on me while I drifted in the middle of the lake. The only thing that was a little disconcerting was the possibility of someone staring and watching. I was comfortable with my body, but the idea still had me turning over and swimming, watching the perimeter. I followed my gut again, which told me to dive under the waterfall.

I followed the familiarity and when I surfaced behind the roar I found a darkened cave. A low rock made it easy to scale and I gripped the wet stone walls for balance as I pulled myself out of the water. I followed my muscle memory further in.

"Hello?" I called into the darkness and an echo called back to me. The low light bounced crazily around the opening as it filtered through the water.

I stepped a little farther into the cave and had the oddest sensation that someone would be waiting for me. I stubbed my toe on a rock and hissed, but my gaze was drawn to a camping lantern. I picked it up and saw that it was wet, but waterproof as well. Twisting the knob, the small lantern lit with a click. The tiny propane flame, shooting light into the shadows. I turned the knob more to grow the flame larger.

The darkness dissipated as I stepped into it with the lantern and walked carefully away from the opening. A creek, just a few inches deep, swelled and flowed from the cave. The roar of the waterfall slowly lessened as the cave turned and grew deeper, and I followed the trail of water back toward its source. There were no additional passages outside of the current path. I wondered if it had been the original path of the river above, before a shift in the earth changed its path.

The roar became a hum and the rock walls vibrated in a way that made them feel alive. After only a few minutes I came to the end of the cave and a deep darkened pool which opened into a cavern, complete with stalactites hanging from the ceiling. Two smaller pools rose above the larger in a flowing stack, as if they'd been created by a genius fountain engineer.

Small openings covered the walls that fed water into the pool from above. The biggest ones looked like a dog could fit through. The sight gave me an odd sensation of being in the middle of an enormous beehive. But instead of honey pouring from them, it was water.

Shivering at the chill in the air I stepped forward and dipped my toe into the pool, curious if it was as cold as the lake. But it wasn't cold at all. It was warm.

The two other, smaller pools fed into the large one and then it created the small creek, which drained into the lake. I lowered myself into the dark pool and reveled in the beauty of the cavern. My body was warmed in moments and I let myself drift again. As I did pictures and sounds seemed to flash into my mind. I tried to hold onto them, to bring them forward to examine, but it was as if someone was flipping through a picture album too quickly and I couldn't get it to stop.

Something told me this place was significant. I just wished I could remember why.

I floated there for a long time, safe and warm.

When my skin began to prune, I got out of the pool and walked with the lantern back to the waterfall. I knew that I could stay for as long as I wanted, but there was a deeper need to find out what the Resistance wanted from me. I walked in the stream of water from the pools, as it kept my feet warm. As I got farther away from the source, it began to run cold. I set the lantern down where I'd found it, turning it off, then dove through the waterfall back into the lake.

I surfaced sputtering, as it now felt frigid compared to the pools I'd left. I half expected Daily to be on the beach waiting next to my clothes, but he wasn't. I felt a small tug of sympathy and pushed it away. I hadn't been unnecessarily cruel. I said what I needed to say in order for him to understand my position.

The idea that I would kiss him when I remembered made me vaguely queasy. As if my entire personality would change upon remembering him.

I quickly made my way out of the pool, then cursed when I realized I didn't have a towel. I picked up my clothes and moved back to my rock, shivering. There I was surprised to find an oversized, fluffy towel. I frowned at it before ignoring it.

He needed to realize that he couldn't buy my affection with small gestures. It was antithetical to who I was as a person. I would bow to no one. The fact that he seemed to know me better than I did myself was deeply unsettling. I felt like a cage was closing around me.

I stood in a patch of sun, which had risen high above the lake. The air, while still cool, was beginning to warm. I pulled my clothes on and left the towel where it was. They stuck to my skin, as it wasn't completely dry yet, but my stomach was telling me I was still hungry and that it was time to go.

I made my way around the lake and back through the woods to the flight platform. I walked unaccosted across the clearing and onto the base. I made a note to mention that their security seemed to be a little lax.

I found the concrete stairs I'd originally exited through and walked back into the mess hall. This time the tables were all full. As soon as I entered the room, however, all noise shut down. My appearance screeched everything to a halt. I sighed as I heard a fork drop from across the room.

"I overheard the statement that everyone needs to be quiet around me," I stated to the room as everyone continued to stare at me. "While I appreciate the gesture, it is wholly unnecessary."

The silence continued.

"If you wish to stay silent, then I will leave that up to you," I continued. "But I think it's my job to know whether or not I can handle something, and it sounds like I've done a damn good job so far."

"Exousia!" A voice shouted from the crowd, then with a short pause the rest followed.

"Exousia! Exousia!" They chanted and I relaxed. It was an old greeting and farewell that I'd used my entire life.

I moved to the food line as the chatter started back up, albeit at a lower level.

The Uniformity had created a new hierarchy, based on the original Greek Democracy and class system. Exousia meant power and authority. When someone from the Uniformity used it, they were paying homage to the overarching authority of the Uniformity. Here, I think it meant something very different.

I filled my tray and left the mess, making my way back to the hospital room I'd vacated earlier. When I found a recently cleaned and sanitized room, I realized I didn't know exactly where I was staying. I looked around the hallway dumbly.

"Need something, Dekka?" Jensen walked around the corner with his ever present clipboard and reached for his pen light.

"If you push that light in my face again, we might have a problem," I raised a brow at him.

"Ok," Jensen grinned and let his hand drop back to his side. "Nice to see your spunk returning."

"Wish I could say the same," I tilted my head as I studied his face. "Did we know each other before?"

"Vaguely," his bottle green eyes flashed. "Would you like me to show you where your cabin is?"

I nodded and he turned on his heels, heading back the way he came.

"This way," he tossed over his shoulder as he turned the corner.

I followed, tray in hand, making sure I didn't spill anything. Jensen moved quickly and was taller than I, so I had to jog to catch up. He led me down a series of halls and out another set of concrete stairs. As soon as we ascended to the top, he pulled out a cigarette and lit it.

"Why is security so lax around this facility?" I asked him.

"It isn't," Jensen responded.

"When I walked to and from the little lake earlier, no one approached me," I pointed out.

"Well they wouldn't," Jensen responded and began walking again, inhaling and exhaling smoke. "They all know who you are."

"The flight vehicles were left unattended," I told him, as I waved away the smoke with one hand and balanced my tray with the other.

"No they weren't."

"How do you know?" I asked.

"Because every inch of our perimeter, and much of the surrounding area, is monitored, either by sentries or surveillance."

"Of course," I shook my head and forced down the embarrassment. "I should have realized."

"No," he continued to walk as I followed. "You did

realize. You were the reason those parameters were implemented in the first place."

"What do you mean?"

"I mean," Jensen stopped suddenly and turned, causing me to nearly smash my food plate on him. He crushed the half smoked cigarette under his boot. "That you took a ragtag group of dumbasses and turned them into a legitimate Resistance, then you left."

Jensen's bottle green eyes flashed again before he turned to continue walking.

"You're mad at me," I stated as I followed again.

The trees closed around us, and the chill of the shadows creeped in.

"How very astute of you."

"I'm not going to apologize for decisions I didn't make, or for not knowing you," I told him.

A dark cabin, snuggled against a moss-covered rock face, came into view.

"I'm not expecting you to," Jensen replied as he walked up the few steps to the porch and opened the screen door, holding it open for me.

"What do you want from me?" I stopped in front of him, forcing him to look at me again.

"I don't want anything from you."

I could tell that was a lie, but I wasn't sure what he was gaining by saying it. I studied him for a moment, and his eyes shifted away. I let it go for now and walked through the open door. The screen banged closed behind me and I turned to see Jensen walking off, back through the woods.

I stood in the darkness for a moment, before finding a small table to set my tray on. I wandered the small cabin and found lanterns and candles. For now, I lit the candles with a box of matches I found on the small table and studied my surroundings.

There was indoor plumbing, which I was thankful for. A small sink and shelves were next to a wide fireplace, which seemed to double for cooking as well as heat, and dominated the small space to the right of the entrance. There was even an old cast iron pot hanging over the area where a fire would be. I shivered as I walked over and took the pot off the hook, then built a fire with the logs and kindling stacked neatly next to it.

Once it was built, I closed the door to keep in the warm and explored the rest of the space. A loft rose above the back wall, which was lined with bookshelves. A ladder was how you gained access to the loft, and its only contents were a large feather bed that lay directly on the ground. Below the loft and behind the wall of books was a small bathroom, complete with clawfoot copper tub/shower. It looked nice enough that I considered relaxing in it, but I'd already spent a good amount of time in the water today.

I walked back out to the living space instead, intent on eating.

I sat at the little wood dining table with matching chairs. The food I'd taken from the mess had begun to look unappetizing, but I knew I needed to eat. So I ate as the fire crackled in the hearth, and I continued to study my surroundings. There were windows, with no coverings, on every wall. I remembered what Jensen said about every inch of the facility being monitored and I made note to look for any cameras or listening devices in here.

There was a fighting dummy in the corner and I knew that I needed to start training again. Undoubtedly my stamina had dropped. I needed to check my reaction times. I wouldn't be any good to the Resistance if I wasn't at my best. My head ached slightly and I pushed the thoughts away. It was hard to believe that I was a part of this, but at this point the Uniformity would never take me back. So it was time to choose a side.

The idea struck me as odd that I'd created this effective Resistance, as it was today. Why had I left? What information had been so important that I'd deemed it necessary to leave? Jensen couldn't be the only one who'd felt abandoned.

Yawning, I pushed up and took my tray to the sink, cleaning it absentmindedly.

When I was finished, I set the tray aside and crawled up the ladder to the feather bed. I needed a nap. I flopped face first onto the bed and drifted off instantly.

My legs shook as I moved to take him deeper. It was never enough. I always wanted more, and he was always willing to give it.I opened for him the way I never had for anyone. I arched my back to give him access to my breasts as our speed increased. The roughness of his palms scraped my nipples in an indescribably sensual way. His clever fingers rubbed and plucked and the sweet ache built. It built until I was frenzied and begging him to go faster.

My back pressed into the rock wall of the warm pool. The darkness around us felt humid and alive as we took each other higher until finally, something burst inside us both. My body rippled with pleasure as I clenched convulsively around him.

"Cass..." The whisper was as warm as the pool and tickled.

"Oh, Jen," I wrapped my arms around him to pull him closer.

My eyes shot open and I sat straight up. The head rush had me grabbing my head and turning over to bury it in my pillow.

I let myself scream. It was muffled, and hurt my head, but I couldn't help myself. An echo of the ache I felt in the memory reverberated through my body, causing my throat to close and my eyes to burn. The sudden need I had for him burned through me and without an outlet, I yelled my frustration. I let out my anger, my exhaustion, my sadness. And when I was done screaming and my voice ran hoarse, I wept.

The sobs scraped out of my throat and ripped me apart

from the inside. The pain and bewilderment of the last... days? Weeks? Months? I realized then, I didn't even know how long it had been since my life had effectively ended. How was I supposed to cope?

My body shook and I kicked off my boots as I realized I'd gone to bed fully dressed. Tears continued to stream as I stripped on the bed and got under the covers naked, trembling and sniffling. I let myself be dragged down by the emotions surrounding me. There was no one to be strong for. Not anymore.

Though the acuity of the pain astonished me, I'd been aware that it was there. I sniffled again and closed my eyes, snuggling into the warmth of my feather bed and I tried to push away the memory that had pushed its way into my subconscious. My breathing slowed and I let myself drift, not quite sleeping for the rest of the night.

When the morning finally came I dressed and pushed the night before out of my mind. There was no real way to tell if it had been an authentic memory. I mean, I hadn't had a seizure as a result. So that could mean it was a dream. Jen could be anyone and, whoever they were, they meant nothing to me now.

I repeated that to myself the entire way to the mess hall. I needed to spend time on my own for a while, so I would scavenge some tools and supplies so I wouldn't have to make a daily trek to the mess. Feeling a bit better, I walked through the trees, projecting a confidence I was struggling to feel.

Of course the first person I ran into was Jensen.

I opened the door to the mess hall and smacked him with it, knocking the tray of food he was carrying out of his hand and onto the floor. His face remained composed, as if resigned to the fate of the food. His eyes connected with mine and my stomach went liquid thinking of the dream memory.

I had the oddest urge to avoid his gaze, but I continued to search his eyes as he did mine. Whatever he saw in mine however, had the corners of his mouth lifting fractionally from his constantly grim features. A light seemed to glow behind his eyes that softened them in a way I hadn't noticed before.

"Was that for me?" I let the door close behind me.

His gaze cut away from mine for a moment to take in the mess on the ground. When his eyes returned to mine, there was humor and embarrassment shining within them. He opened his mouth to answer, but it shut abruptly and the glow that had started dimmed.

"Good morning," Daily walked over to us and I continued to stare at Jensen, though he now avoided my gaze. He held a tray in his hands, though I couldn't see exactly what in my periphery.

"Can you two answer me something?" I looked to Daily for a moment before redirecting back at Jensen. "Why is it that you two are permitted to look like men, but nearly everyone else has a shaved head and gender non-binary clothing?"

"Because we are known," Jensen answered before Daily could. "I have a job as a medical assistant in the city. I'm on leave right now."

"And I was your handler, so I always found employment near you," Daily grinned at me and offered the tray, which I took. "People would notice and wonder if we wore wigs or identity concealing clothing. The soldiers have been trained to infiltrate and adopt the local customs of all ten territories. Sometimes that means being more binary to blend."

"It's a standard you implemented as part of the overarching goal of the resistance," Jensen supplied quietly. "The idea and goal that binary gender is an extremely antiquated philosophy. So as a neutral there are no men versus women, just people. Only humans."

I looked around the room at the people laughing, eating, and existing in a way I'd never seen before. The truth of the words he spoke resonated with me in a way I couldn't describe. I realized I felt exactly that way, but had never been able to put it into words.

Obviously, I had at some point.

"Let's sit," Jensen motioned to a small table nearby.

I moved, set the tray down and began picking at some of the food. I suddenly wasn't as hungry as I'd been moments ago. I felt like I was on a precipice looking into a void, seeing that the other side was within jumping distance, but not being able to remember how to jump.

"What is my part in all of this?" I looked from Jensen to Daily.

One seemed reserved, the other eager to answer.

"You are the Stratego," Daily smiled as he said this.

"How can I be the Strat?" I demanded. "You're telling me that I left the uppermost position of the Resistance to go undercover?"

"Yes," Jensen confirmed, a deep seated bitterness seeming to spew from that one word.

"There was no one else with your prospects," Daily defended. "You had the best chance to get as high as possible and gain the most information."

"Do we have other operatives?"

"Yes," Jensen answered again, but this time he sounded tired.

I absentmindedly ate a bite of food while I processed this new horror.

Not only had I, apparently, single-handedly created this active arm of the Resistance, I also decided to leave it. Was I bored? What had my motivations been?

"You did give us an enormous amount of information," Jensen said quietly. "However, the issue we ran into when you were gone, was our command. We didn't split, but there have been factions that were becoming louder as they objected."

"Yes," Daily confirmed, placidly. "Most of these people joined the Resistance because of you, and there was a feeling of abandonment."

"Who is the Taxi?"

"Umm..." Daily's eyes shifted away.

I looked to Jensen, who looked as resigned as when I knocked the tray from his hands.

"Is it the same person that I would have installed when I left?"

"No," Jensen said. "And before you ask, I can't tell you right now."

"Why?" I demanded.

"Because you are still healing," Jensen's hand twitched as if he wanted to reach out, but it stayed on the table. "This is something that will need to wait until you regain more of your memories."

"Is there a way we can speed that up?" I wanted to know.

"There are a few," Jensen frowned. "But it is better for you if they come back gradually. You could risk a massive aneurysm otherwise."

I huffed and stood, leaving my tray mostly untouched.

"Ok," I frowned at both of them. "I'm going to be getting some supplies and sequestering myself for a while. It seems easier if I'm alone when the memories come back."

I felt a flush creeping up my neck as I remembered the dream memory from the night before again.

"I can help," Daily stood quickly, eager.

"No," I said, firmly. "I appreciate it, but I need to be alone for a while. Are there phones or communicators here?"

"Yes," Jensen stood as well. "There are old rotary phones that link to cabins and housing areas. They don't use electricity and can't be traced by outside lines. There are a few that you've managed to install in some of the houses of the Uniformity in this area. If found, people assume they are an old artifact so they seemed to be the perfect way to communicate. You will find yours in the cabin's kitchen."

"Good," I moved my shoulders to stretch them. "I'll see you around."

I walked away from the table and toward the large kitchen, separated from the mess hall by silver swinging doors. Instead of bursting through, as had already become a habit, I opened the door gently so as not to knock anyone else over. When I saw that no one was directly in my path, I pushed the door open wide and let it swing closed behind me.

I surveyed the long spartan metal prep tables and the few soldiers that remained, cleaning after the morning rush. They talked quietly amongst themselves as I grabbed a collapsible basket and began to fill it with supplies. Just enough for a few days. I avoided the meat, as I wouldn't short the kitchen in order to feed myself. I could hunt or fish if I needed it.

That errant thought caught me off guard.

I knew I could hunt in theory, as it was a part of basic training. But the confidence of the statement to myself denoted not just a theoretical experience. I gathered supplies quickly, nodded at the soldiers who were brave enough to look up, then left the way I'd come.

I knew what I needed to do with my time.

Nearly running, I burst into the cabin. I set the supplies in the kitchen and let my instincts guide me as I found a backpack. I kept it light with emergency supplies, a distress beacon, and three knives of varying sizes and serrations. A collapsible fishing pole and some freeze dried protein bars, a canteen and a small water purifier. Without a second thought, I left the cabin and continued on foot.

At first I thought I was going back to my lake but then I veered away, farther up the mountain, rather than toward the launch pad. I saw as I continued upward that the flight area was not the top of the mountain, but a small flat expanse in the side of the mountain near the top. It was almost as high as the peak, but it surrounded the expanse.

Upward I hiked, climbing at times as the terrain dictated. The invisible force that pushed me encouraged me to move faster. I slipped and nearly lost my balance, but recovered quickly. I could see the top of the rise and ran, flat out. The chilled wind on my face felt exhilarating.

I'd left the trees far behind, as the top had become barren like a desert. The dirt was soft and dark. I approached the edge with caution and looked down into the crater that hid our little resistance.

A dormant volcano. I didn't remember learning that information, but I knew it.

Of course. That explained the hot springs. I sidled right up to the edge of the sheer cliff that presided over the hidden camp. I'd found the topmost part of the crater and realized why I hadn't noticed before. There was thick foliage inside the round rising walls that leant the assumption that it was a forest. The sides of the crater rose in varying degrees, most of them low. More than half of the walls had crumbled into themselves, making the single living rock face on which I now stood. The rest were barely hills, easily scaled, as if this were the peak that had originally existed before the eruption that would have decimated the area a hundreds of years ago.

I sat at the edge and dangled my feet over. The sky above me had cleared of the lingering overcast skies and shone bright blue. The forest stretched out below me in all directions, a sea of green that dissected the horizon. There were a few breaks in the trees that I now recognized as the Resistance base of operations. I looked farther down the slope and located where the ReConditioning camp would be. I was about to look away when I saw a flicker of movement.

I squinted and waited for more, but there was nothing. I leaned forward, as if that would help me see.

"Cas!" I felt a hand on my shoulder from behind me and nearly lost my balance.

I grabbed the hand on my shoulder and forced away the instinct to use my momentum to throw them over my shoulder, which would have sent us both over the cliff. I looked over my shoulder into Daily's worried and frustrated eyes. The sharp blue was almost as bright as the sky, which seemed to be reflected in them. They reminded me painfully of my nightmares and something clicked. My stomach did a flip as our gazes connected and I realized that he was the only thing between me and certain death. Something dark moved behind his eyes as he seemed to come to the same conclusion.

I smiled hugely and batted my eyes at him. Maybe I was too hasty throwing away the farce earlier.

"Thank you so much!" I said breathily and began to move my chest like I was breathing hard. I reached across to my shoulder and gripped his wrist, so that both of my hands held his. "I can't believe I was so dumb. I could have died."

I forced out an awkward laugh as he smiled hesitantly, and whatever had been behind his eyes dissolved as he helped me to my feet. I pretended to stumble into his arms, which put him off balance and moved us both further from the cliff's edge. Once we were a safe distance I released a breath I hadn't realized I'd been holding.

"What were you doing?"

I ignored the censure in his tone and forced myself to look into his eyes, which expressed genuine concern. I let a small amount of the fear that I felt show. It had been stupid of me to let my guard down and leave my back open to any number of enemies. I threaded my fingers behind his neck, giving myself easy access to a number of pressure points, all while seeming casual. I let a slow smile spread over my lips before answering.

"I was looking at where the old ReConditioning camp

used to be," I looked back over my shoulder, exposing my throat and leaning back against his arms, which still encircled my waist.

In my periphery I could see that his gaze tracked down the length of me, rather than following my own. I needed to know if what I saw in his eyes was something to be concerned about. I looked back to him and pretended not to notice his brazenness.

"Daily," I moved out of his arms, feigning embarrassment and putting my arms behind my back, his grip on my waist tightened possessively for a moment before letting me go. "I want to apologize for my behavior the other day. I was overwhelmed and needed to vent. You were just the handiest person available."

"I'm always here when you need me," Daily chuckled and stepped forward as if to hold me again but I dodged under his arms out of reach, picking up my pack. I tried not to choke on the lies I was spewing, but I couldn't let him corner me against the cliff again.

"For anything," he continued.

His gaze heated and my stomach turned, this time in revulsion. I couldn't put my finger on it, but something wasn't right with him. I could tell I was attracted to him on a very base level, but something about his behavior had me keeping my distance rather than trying to get to know him. I pulled on my pack and smiled brightly.

Trust yourself. The secret message came back to me.

"Do you know if the ReConditioning camp is still running?" I asked, remembering the movement that had me leaning over the cliff to begin with.

"In a way," Daily smiled darkly and the way he said it had me shifting to the balls of my feet.

"In a way?" I prompted.

"We infiltrated the camp while you were going there," Daily's smile turned triumphant. "It has been our own personal recruitment camp for years."

"Genius," I relaxed as I looked back toward where the old camp was located.

"Of course," Daily looked a little sad. "It was your idea. And you supplied us with recruits while you were training your own."

I looked back at him confused.

"Since you were a sleeper, you wouldn't even realize it when you sent people to the camp," Daily shrugged. "You would write a recommendation for ReConditioning with this specific place in mind. Then, depending on their loyalty, we would either keep them here if it was questionable, or send them off to infiltrate."

"How many?" I wondered. "How many sleepers are there?"

"Hundreds," Daily shrugged. "I'm sure there is a recorded number, somewhere."

"Huh," I turned back to Daily and beamed. "Well I've got to be going. I'm practicing my solo hunting and fishing."

I shaded my eyes and looked up at the position of the sun.

"I've got to get going if I want to start tracking anything before dark."

"You want company?"

"Thanks, but no," I held my breath, so that color bloomed in my cheeks like a blush. "I'm testing my limits and I need to be alone. You never know, maybe I'll remember something while I'm hiking."

"Yeah," Daily nodded, but I could tell he wasn't as happy with that answer as I thought he would be. "I'll see you later."

"See you," I waved and started off.

As soon as I got to the covering of the trees, I moved as quickly as I was physically able. I made my way down the cliff, opposite the way I'd come, then curled back around to my original trail. I followed the signs of my own passing then hooked a low thick branch, scaling it as quickly as possible.

The pine needles were thick and offered a lot of cover. I couldn't see far in either direction, but I could see the trail I'd come from directly below me. I calmed my breathing and sat perfectly still, waiting.

By my count, it took more than thirty minutes before I heard footfalls from the same way I'd come. Daily passed directly under me and continued on without pausing. His pace was mellow, but he was definitely following me. I made a mental note to be more careful about not leaving a trail next time.

I waited another thirty minutes after his footfalls receded to descend. I brushed the pine needles from my hair and shoulders then backtracked to the other side of the cliff again. I continued on from the point I'd turned, making sure to leave no trace this time.

 It took me approximately two days to start feeling guilty that I hadn't checked in.

I spent my days listening to my surroundings, doing my best to leave no trace, and sleeping in trees. I always walked in a large arching circle before ending back where I started in order to climb a tree and set up my hammock high in its boughs. I slept lightly, surrounded by the feeling of promnesia.

I'd done all of this before, perhaps even in these same trees.

A crack that reverberated through the woods had me crouching. I kept low as I moved toward the sound and pulled a large hunting knife from the sheath at my hip. I'd bagged a few small game with traps, which I'd skinned and salted so they would hold over for another day. The traps I'd set had felt like remembering how to breathe. It had been so natural to plot out a course around the tree I'd designated for that night's camp so that I could pull the game that had been snared.

Identifying the saplings that could be used was so familiar that I could hear my own voice as I taught others the same, though it had never been a part of my syllabus at University. The only subject I'd taught that had even come close to this had been tracking in an urban environment. As I set traps and released them, the memories became clearer. I breathed deeply through them, but I didn't have a seizure or any timeloss.

There was one particular memory that swam through my head repeatedly.

I walked through a forest very similar to this. My small hand gripped in a larger one. They towered over me, but I wasn't afraid. In fact, I was content. I enjoyed hearing the deep rumble of a laugh when I asked questions too quickly, before he could answer the first one.

"My precious," he would say. "I will answer all of your

questions. But you need to be patient."

"How?" I demanded.

Every day he had laughed off the demand, until this day. He looked at me seriously and nodded.

"I will show you," he gripped my hand tighter and we veered off the cut path of the forest and walked up an incline until we found a creek.

He crouched low and smiled into my eyes.

"When you find a small run of water, you will be led to a larger body," he told me. "In order to find your patience, you must seek this out."

"Why?" My childish voice pouted.

"Because, baby," he stood again but his gaze never wavered. "The sounds of larger bodies of water will drown out your mind."

The man turned and we walked in silence as I contemplated what he said.

"Will this help me remember you when you're gone?" I wondered aloud.

"It might," his voice sounded sad.

"I don't want to forget you."

"I don't want you to forget me either," he replied. "But you have a full and important life ahead of you. I would only be holding you back."

"I don't think that's true," though it was the voice of a child, it was fierce in its defiance.

"Neither do I."

The matter-of-fact declaration had surprised us both into silence again and I remembered holding back tears. I didn't want to lose this man.

"Ah," the brightness in his voice returned and I was able to push back the emotions as we found a roaring river. "Here we are."

"It's so loud," I yelled and clamped my hands over my ears.

"The sound will help until you know how to center

yourself and find your patience, your stillness," he crouched and spoke directly into my ear. "Find a rock big enough for us both to sit with our legs crossed."

I did. We walked along the river for a time until we found a large flat boulder that could fit both of us. I scrambled to the top and sat. He followed suit and crossed his legs under him when he sat, keeping his back straight and laying his hands on his knees. I immediately mimicked the posture.

"Take a deep breath and close your eyes," he said loud enough for me to hear over the moving water below. "Breathe deep and listen to the water. Listen to it until it fills your mind and everything else falls away."

I did as he asked, but it was hard at first. I struggled, fidgeted. Thought about my friends, games we played. I would sneak peeks at the man next to me to see what he was doing. Each time he sat there, unmoving, with his eyes closed. I decided to try again.

I breathed deeply and pulled the sound into my mind. I wasn't sure how long we'd been there when I felt a hand on my shoulder. I opened my eyes and saw that the sun was beginning to dip low.

"You did it, baby," he smiled down at me and I nodded.

I felt good, energized, as if I'd been sleeping. My mind was quiet as it had never been before and I smiled up at him.

The memory faded there, with glimpses of the same man teaching me hunting, camping and many other traditions that had been passed down from his family.

My family.

Though I tried, I could never see the man's face. It was fuzzy, as if his identity was intentionally withheld. There were other parts of him that were crystal clear. Like his wide hands, towering height, and dark skin. And his laugh.

A thrill ran up my spine as it played over in my mind.

He was the one who had taught me to be still.

I continued gathering my prey and began making the trek back to camp. I hadn't wandered too far so I knew I would be back before nightfall.

I secured my kills to my belt and gathered all of my supplies.

It took six hours to hike back up the mountain and into the camp. This time I saw the sentries and sent them nods as they saluted when I passed. Word must have travelled that I was heading back to camp, because Daily was there to greet me as I entered the mess.

Dinner was well underway, but I got some excited looks as I brought in my haul. A couple of soldiers let out a whoop when they saw the meat. Daily stood with his back to the kitchen and barred my way, arms crossed.

I stared him down.

He relented with a sigh and opened the door for me.

I dumped the carcasses on the drain rack next to the sink that was used for cleaning game indoors. It was only used for small game, because there was a larger one for deer and elk outside.

I paused, realizing that had been an unbidden piece of knowledge. I smiled to myself as I began to clean and skin the game. I set the pelts aside for later use.

"You don't have anything to say for yourself?" Daily demanded from behind me.

"What should I say?" I looked over my shoulder for a moment and noticed that a few of the kitchen workers had slowed and seemed to be listening to the exchange.

Daily still stood there with his arms crossed.

"You abandoned us," Daily's voice was close to a whine. "You could have been hurt."

I paused for a moment and considered my blood soaked hands, before continuing without comment. If he truly knew me, then he knew my skill set for the outdoors and would have known I was in no danger. I wondered again who this self-proclaimed lover was. I know that I had told myself that I could trust him on the video, but something felt off.

Daily huffed and then seemed to gather himself. He

stepped forward and placed his hands on either side of my hips on the sink, not technically touching me, and whispered in my ear.

"I'm sorry," his voice was deep and sultry. "I was just worried for you. I need you safe. I've lost you so many times, I just want you to stay put."

His words worked down my spine in a shiver. A flame seemed to kindle in my stomach and I had the strange urge to push backward into him. To lay my head on his shoulder and bare my neck to him.

I fumbled the blade I held. In trying to catch it, I sliced my palm and broke the spell that had taken hold.

I hissed in pain, and threw my head back. It caught Daily directly in the nose and he stumbled back into a steel prep table swearing, holding the bent cartilage that gushed blood. Someone dropped something and it clanged loudly in my head. I pushed my hand under the running water and saw the deep slice for what it was.

I needed to staunch the blood.

I grabbed a nearby towel that looked mostly clean and wrapped it. Daily continued to curse, pulling his nose up and attempting to do the same. I grabbed an additional towel as my hand was already bleeding through the first and made a fist around it.

As if summoned Jensen walked in, a distracted look on his face that turned quickly to confusion, then hopeful humor.

"Finally punch him?" He asked me.

"No," Daily's voice was deeply nasal as he attempted to answer for me.

"Headbutt actually," I smiled wanly as his smile grew into a grin. Woozy, I leaned precariously and nearly lost my balance.

"I think I need to sit," I said, as dark rings around my eyes began to close in.

Another curse, this one from Jensen, as I felt myself crumple to the ground.

"Intense physical strain and blood loss," Jensen's voice related to someone else in the room. "I'm not sure how she cut her hand since she's usually so good with knives. She will need NuSkin."

I felt like I was detached from the rest of my body.

"She probably wasn't paying attention," a voice that was so deeply familiar that I knew this had to be a dream, even if it was tinged with a deep bitterness I'd never heard in it before. "Typical."

Golden eyes swam in my mind and began to sink back into the darkness.

I tried to reach out, but my hands were strapped down. Then everything hurt, burned for an instant, before it was gone and I drifted deeper. The voices were harder to concentrate on, so I let myself float on my little lake.

When my eyes blinked open I stared at the ceiling for a time, then Jensen shined his ever present penlight in my eyes. I blinked in irritation.

"Reactive and equal," he muttered.

When my eyes refocused, I looked into his and saw exhaustion. I looked around and saw that I was still in the kitchen. For someone who had never lost consciousness during training, this was beginning to be a very uncomfortable habit. It made me feel weak.

"Were we together?" I asked bluntly.

Surprised, he blinked as if I'd shined a light in his own eyes.

"Uhh," his eyes cut across the room then back to me.

I turned my head to follow his line of sight and saw Daily sleeping in a chair, his nose stuffed with cotton and a bandage over the bridge.

"Why does it matter if he's here," I narrowed my eyes when I turned back to face him. "Did I cheat on him?"

"No," a deep rage seemed to burn suddenly behind his eyes. "You cheated on me."

With that, he turned and left the room.

I shut my mouth, as it had begun to hang open, and stared at the empty doorway.

I continued to stare, until my hand twinged and I realized I still needed treatment. I looked to where Daily had been in the chair, then to a swinging back door where he'd left through.

My eyes wandered to the staff and saw the questioning eyes that quickly turned away as they made contact. I made a tighter fist with my hand and kept the towel where it was, wrapped around my hand.

"You," I pointed with my uninjured hand at the closest cook.

They turned silently toward me and cocked their head in question. The deep brown eyes that connected with mine radiated calm and kindness.

"Finish cleaning these," I gestured toward the game. "Set three aside for me, the rest can go into the community pot."

The silent cook beamed as a slow smile bloomed and they nodded.

I turned quickly as my hand began to throb and headed the way Daily had left. I didn't particularly want to find him, but I didn't want to leave through the mess. I needed to find some supplies, and maybe another set of hands for the stitches.

The doorway led to the hallway outside the mess. I walked quickly to where I knew the medical area was from this point. I could stitch it up myself if I had to, but I didn't particularly want to, as it wouldn't be very pretty.

My mind spun and I lost my balance. I tripped and knocked into the nearest wall. A memory tore at my mind, I saw myself sewing up my own side. A cut? No, a puncture. I'd been hiking and I'd fallen. An errant branch had pierced my side. I'd had a basic first aid kit and added fishing line and needles, just in case.

My stomach pitched at the memory. The pain had been searing. My hands had been sticky with my own blood, shaking from the adrenaline and blood loss. My vision faded in and out, then I vomited. I cursed as I sewed. I'd passed out with the needle still in my hand, waking up sometime later to a snuffling nearby.

A white wolf sniffed my side.

"Aurora!" A male voice nearby called. "Where'd you go?"

The wolf's tongue lolled out as it looked at me in some form of happy grin, then bounded off yipping toward the voice.

I groaned as I attempted to sit up. My throat was so dry it hurt to swallow.

"Alright," the affable voice came. "What'd you find this time?"

The yipping got closer again, then I heard a gasp.

"Miss!" The voice ran toward me as I tried to stand. "What happened?"

"A misstep," I fell back and gasped at the shooting pain.

"Here," he crouched down and offered his arms. "Let me carry you."

"No," I attempted to wave him off. "I can do it."

I looked over into his eyes, a green I'd never seen outside of old pictures of glass. It shone in the dappled light around us and my stomach turned over again in one slow roll. I leaned over and vomited again, then weakly tried to wipe my mouth.

"I'll try not to take that personally," came the response. "Where did you come from?"

"The camp," I told him and when I tried to sit up again, he scooped me into his arms.

His strength surprised me, so that I gripped around his neck.

"I told you," I frowned as he began walking. "I can do it."

"I know," his voice came happily. "But you would probably die trying to drag yourself down there."

The dog danced and jumped around us, thinking this was some kind of game.

"But my gear..." I said lamely.

"I'm sure you'll be up hiking again in no time."

"I can't let anyone see you carrying me," I sighed, though I was secretly enjoying it.

"It'll be our little secret," he whispered.

"Is that a real wolf?" I asked, looking at the happily trailing dog.

"Mostly," he nodded.

"Won't you get in trouble going to the camp?"

"I work there," he smiled.

"I've never seen you before," I challenged.

"No, you wouldn't have, Miss. I work in the infirmary."

"They let you be a nurse?" I asked, astounded.

"No," he chuckled. "I'm a glorified orderly, and they parade me out to test the girls they are sending home."

His head turned to mine and the light in them reflected brightly.

Too soon, we entered an empty infirmary, as he had somehow been able to get onto the grounds unchallenged. He lay me on a bed and washed his hands, then the wound. He handed me another cloth so I could clean myself up.

"I'll go get a doctor," he stood to leave, but I suddenly didn't want him to go.

"Wait," I said and he paused. "I..."

I struggled to find a reason for him to stay, grabbing the first thing that came to mind.

"They won't let me go hiking again on my own if they see this," I gestured toward the wound. "It didn't hurt anything internally, I just need a few stitches. Can you get me the supplies? I'll do it myself."

He turned and looked at me, then the wound. A smirk tugged at the corner.

"You call that sewing?"

I looked down and saw the jagged pieces sewn awkwardly.

"Ok," he sighed. "I'll do it. You'll be liable to pass out again."

"I said I could do it," I pressed as he went around the room gathering the needed supplies.

Aurora sat patiently near the door, watching.

"Again," he replied. "I'm sure you can. I don't doubt your willpower at all. I've seen you around. You're very commanding."

"You've seen me around?" My heart thrilled at the idea that he'd seen me.

"Yes," he nodded. "And I know you've seen me too."

"No I haven't," confused, I shook my head.

"Not at camp," he walked back over and set out the supplies. "At the lake."

My jaw dropped as I realized what he meant, and my face flamed.

"Embarrassed?" He chuckled as he used a pair of scissors to cut the current set of stitches. "I didn't think that was possible with the way you'd been watching me."

"You knew I was there?" My mind whirled as I replayed the naked boy who'd swam at the lake then disappeared.

"Of course," he shrugged as I groaned in pain while he worked. "You were sitting on a rock directly in the path of the sun. I'm not blind."

"Then why did you..." I couldn't finish the question.

"Get naked for you?" He finished.

I nodded weakly.

"Because you're the only one who hadn't noticed me," his chuckle became a bit self-deprecating. "And I needed to see if you were as cold as you appeared. So I followed you one day."

I shifted as much as I was able, uncomfortable with the idea that someone had been watching me without my knowledge.

"Finished," he stood and cleaned up his area. "I'll grab some clothes from the lost and found for you so you can toss those. Then I would suggest just staying put. I'll log your visit as severe cramping, so you can stay for a few hours. Then I would suggest staying in your bunk for at least a day before going out again."

I looked down at my side and saw the tiny formal stitches, artfully done. I looked back at him and nodded.

"What's your name?" I asked, suddenly.

"Jen," he replied, blinking. "Jensen."

"It's nice to meet you, Jensen," I smiled at him, and repeated something he'd said earlier. "Our little secret."

I came out of the memory with a throbbing head. Somehow I'd managed to keep standing, though I nearly pitched forward. White and shaky, I continued to walk, though slowly. I needed to find someone to help stitch my hand.

You cheated on me, Jensen's voice repeated in my head.

What the hell had he meant? From all accounts, I'd been with Daily from the beginning. Or had I?

A flash of a naked male body diving into the lake as I sat on a warm rock.

Hadn't that been Daily? But Jensen had just confirmed it had been him. And I'd been with him in the hot springs. Someone was lying to me. And I hated being lied to.

I needed to get to the bottom of this, but first I needed to fix my hand.

I walked past empty rooms with medical equipment and gurneys. I kept walking until I heard voices.

"...need to be careful," said a deeply exhausted voice.

I slowed my pace as I heard the tail end of that sentence.

"I'm trying," Daily's voice floated out. "I just don't understand why she doesn't remember me. Is there a way we can force it again?"

"Are you saying we should risk her life?" The anger in the voice that responded sounded so familiar that my heart nearly broke at the sound.

I edged forward to hear more.

"I'm saying that she's useless to us like this," Daily

replied. "She's spending her time hunting instead of in the war room, where she belongs."

"And by war room, you mean with you," the voice became irate. "Look, we did this together, but something is different this time. What did you do?"

"Nothing!" Daily said defensively. "I just want her back. Besides you were so close before she came back."

"And yet, you're the one who brought her back," the voice returned. "Things were going just fine without her here. We've been making progress."

"I couldn't leave her there to die," Daily stated.

"It may have been better all around."

"You don't mean that."

"And yet, you want to try and ReCondition her again," the voice chuckled darkly. "You know the risks as well as I. Are you saying you'd rather her die than be with *him*?"

"Don't pretend like you wouldn't prefer that," Daily's reply startled me and I began to back away as the voices seemed to come closer to the doorway.

Adrenaline shot through me as I realized something was very, very wrong. I squeezed my injured palm to make sure it wasn't a dream, or some sort of living memory. Something told me I knew the other person in that room, but it felt impossible. She died. She was dead. I quietly slipped into the empty room next to the one I'd been listening outside of. Leaving the door open, I heard them mutter a few more things before walking in different directions.

Had they been talking about me? There was no other conclusion. As my head and hand pounded, my heart raced. I walked around the room and gathered the supplies I needed. I knew now that I could trust no one here, not even myself.

Once I'd gathered the things I needed I left the way I'd come, scanning the hallway for Daily. I went straight to my cabin and laid out the supplies and cleaned my hand, grunting as it stung and pulled. I thought about everything as I worked.

Should I tell Jensen? Can I trust him? What would I tell him?

When I finished, I took a hot shower and let my muscles relax. My mind was so full, that I dried off and crawled into my loft bed naked, not bothering with clothes. Thankfully, I fell quickly and deeply into a dreamless sleep.

I woke because of the throbbing in my hand. I pushed through it. I knew taking a pain blocker would cut the pain, but I also knew that it would dull my overall senses. Medicine was a switch off and at the moment I would rather feel the pain and be switched on. I blinked my gritty eyes and rolled over.

At the sound of pots and pans in my kitchen clanging I rolled off the bed silently, cursing myself. How had I missed the door opening? I made a mental note to rig some sort of sound around the entry points. I knew it was unlikely that anyone in my kitchen meant me harm, but still I moved, naked and silent, to look over the side of the loft.

I stared as I watched Jensen walking around my kitchen, completely at home and making something that was beginning to smell heavenly. I stood and leaned against the banister.

"Why are you here?"

As if startled, he dropped the egg he was holding and it cracked on the floor. He sighed and looked up, then paused as he realized my state of dress.

I raised a brow when he looked away quickly.

"I'm here to apologize," he cleared his throat as he stooped to clean up the egg.

"For what?"

"For storming off yesterday," he sighed and dumped the wasted egg into the trash.

His gaze tracked up and slowly took in my body this time, and I did my best to suppress the shiver that thrilled up my spine. It felt as if he was touching me and a part me remembered, keenly, how it felt to be touched by his hands.

A smile spread on my lips slowly as I watched him look at me. When his gaze finally reached my eyes, his eyes shone like green fire and this time I did shiver.

"I suppose I should put some clothes on," I smirked, instantly regretting it when the fire in his eyes died.

"You probably should," Jensen looked away and continued preparing food.

I sighed and grabbed the first thing on hand to cover up, feeling more irritated than I had the right to. I slipped a long tank over my head, it drifted lightly over my hips and ended about mid thigh. Dressed enough, I climbed down the ladder and sat at the small table, entertaining myself while he moved about the space with familiarity.

More than likely, the other cabins were similarly laid out. Sans lab coat, he walked around in old and worn forest camouflage cargo pants and a fitted green t-shirt that stretched tightly over well honed muscles.

"Why are you here?" My heart picked up as he turned with two plates, piled with pancakes.

"I told you," he stepped forward and set the food in front of me.

"Yes," I nodded as my mouth watered at the site of my favorite breakfast. "But I want to know the real reason."

I dragged my eyes away from the pancakes and toward him as he set another plate in front of himself and sat.

"You could have easily apologized to me the next time you saw me," I said. "So I repeat, why are you here, breaking into my private quarters and making breakfast?"

"It's hardly breaking in, when you leave the front door unlocked," a look of confusion crossed his face for a moment, then slid away. "Honestly, I was more than a little surprised to find it not only unlocked, but missing any sort of sound alerts."

"Honestly," I paused and picked up a fork. "So am I."

"It would make sense if you had someone over," Jensen cleared his throat and focused on his food. "As would your state of dress."

I laughed outright.

"Are you asking whether I slept with someone last night and they snuck out this morning?"

Jensen didn't reply, merely poured an obnoxious amount

of syrup on his stack.

"Well, I didn't," I flexed my hand and felt uncomfortable. "Not that I would have to defend myself if I did."

"Of course not," Jensen hurriedly agreed. "Look, maybe this was a mistake."

He stood to leave.

"Probably," I said and waved my injured hand, which wasn't holding the fork, toward his plate. "You should take your food though. I appreciate you making me breakfast, I just have no idea what you want from me."

"Your hand," he frowned at it and I blinked.

"Yeah?"

"You did that dressing yourself didn't you?"

"Yeah," I shrugged.

"You will never learn," exasperated, he sat back down and began to eat. "Eat your food, then I'm going to dress that wound properly. It would be a shame to let this go to waste."

"Like you dressed my wound when you found me," I asked. "The first time we met?"

Jensen paused, with a bite halfway to his mouth, then proceeded without comment.

When he was finished he stood, took the plate to the sink, and washed his hands. Gathering supplies, he pulled his chair over to my side as I struggled to keep bites of the sodden food on my fork one handed.

When Jensen set down gauze, scissors, tape and the other supplies he'd gathered, I felt my stomach drop. I was suddenly no longer hungry.

"How much have you remembered?" Jensen didn't make eye contact and he held out a hand for mine.

"Not much," I tried to ignore the tingling in my hand as I set it in his. "Enough to be questioning who I can trust."

"Understandably," Jensen carefully unwrapped my hand and I winced as the dried blood and bad stitching pulled. "I would tell you that you can trust me, that there was a time we were closer than either of us could have imagined, but that won't matter to you. Not until you remember on your own, and as we both know, trying to force those memories can be dangerous."

"Is my sister alive?"

Jensen fumbled the scissors he'd picked up, then continued.

"I think we may need to go for a walk when I'm done here," Jensen looked up this time and into my eyes.

Something in his expression pleaded with me to steer away from that line of questioning, but I didn't really want to. So instead of asking direct questions, I rambled about my home life when I was growing up as he worked.

"When I was a child I knew I was attracted to men," I let a small smile play on my lips as I closed my eyes against the painful tugging on my hand. "I'm sure I've told you all of this before, if we were as close as you say we were. So bare with me while I reminisce, because to me this is the first time I've told anyone."

I could feel his nod, even though my eyes remained closed and attempted to relax into my role as storyteller.

"My sister was born when I was five," I told him. "I remember it very clearly. Because of memories like these, I've always been confident in my recall... until recently."

I paused as I let myself see it.

"My mom didn't carry either of us," I sighed. "She'd chosen to go barren, as was her right. There are plenty of women who enjoy going through the motions of pregnancy, but don't necessarily want to take care of children. Or they realize that they can't be a mother.

"As it happens, it's something I always agreed with in regards to the Uniformity," I opened my eyes and let my head rest on the back of the chair, studying the ceiling. "Something that was a large improvement of past social services, something that was created around a lack of social judgement. It actually rewards people for their knowledge of self.

"I mean, that's a scary thing, realizing that you aren't

meant to be a mother, especially after you've already brought a child into this world. Feeling a connection to that life before it's born, and then having it disappear after the child lets out its first gulping scream."

I shook my head as my eyes began to water, feeling Jensen pause as his hands shook for a heartbeat then steadied. I blinked the burning of my eyes back and pushed on. I had no idea where the emotion had come from.

"The fact that the Uniformity gives everyone what they need to be their best self is what drove my loyalty to them. Want to be a mom, but you need some extra help? Pair you with someone who is terrified of pregnancy, but wants to experience motherhood. Want to have a baby, but don't know how you're going to take care of it? Find a perfect home and you can visit. Don't want to procreate at all? No judgement.

"My mom wasn't a birther, but she had all of the love and the time, so she chose to take on kids." I sighed and thought for a moment. "I can respect that. Honestly, if I were to get pregnant I would be terrified that it would be a boy. Part of why I got my tubes tied."

Jensen's hand jerked for a moment, then was steady. If he was unaware, then it was something I'd decided on my own. For some reason I was relieved that it had been my own decision.

"I consider it brave to take on children," I continued. "They take so much time and effort. Plus, there's no guarantee that they won't be psychopaths."

Jensen chuckled as I'd intended and I relaxed again into the story.

"When I returned to my mother's house after I'd gone through Reconditioning, I knew that I was missing parts of my memory, but I just assumed that was what happened when you went through it. And that was why no one really knew what happened at the camps, just that people were different when they returned.

"I walked in and Chastity flew into my arms, and for a

moment it was like I'd never left. Though I could see the change in her figure and her face, she acted like I'd just come back from the store. Then things just progressed like normal, as if I'd never gone away. Until I went to University."

Jensen was done with my hand so I sat forward and leaned on the table as I considered how to continue.

"I never told anyone that I was losing time," I said this while looking into his eyes and watched the hurt pass through them. "I kept it to myself because I didn't want it to affect my chances at landing in the Protectorate. And... to be honest, I was terrified about what I was doing while I was out of it."

I leaned forward and lay my head in my hands as I relived the terror.

"There were girls that just up and went missing, you know," I laughed. "Now at least I know where they went. I would make friends and then suddenly they would be gone. And it was only around me that the disappearances happened. They did end up here, right?"

"You supplied many people for the Resistance," something went through Jensen's eyes, but he nodded. "Though, not all of them made it through training. Most of them could be Reconditioned."

"What happened to the ones that couldn't?" I wanted to know.

"Finish your story and you may know the answer," Jensen prodded gently. "Answers given are harder to believe than answers discovered."

I grumbled in frustration before rolling my neck on my shoulders.

"One week, during vacation, I came home as a surprise and found my sister arguing with my mother. She was saying some awful things about never wanting to be a doctor, which she was being groomed for, and wanting to be an artist instead," my chest grew tight with the memory. "I wanted to wring her neck. How dare she flout the gift she'd been given? How dare she ignore everything that was handed to her? She had a role to fill and she would by Goddess fill it."

My hands shook as my adrenaline surged, just as it had then.

"The next thing I knew I was on the phone, and someone said a date and time before hanging up. I didn't remember even dialing the phone. My mother came in and started screaming at me. She'd just received a notification from those who ran the Reconditioning camp, and that I'd just reported Chastity to them. She was livid. That was when I started screaming back at her, all the anger over my missing memories came boiling out.

"How could I? HOW COULD I?! How could she? Of course she gave me the same bullshit about not having a choice. That she wouldn't have sent me if it had been avoidable. My mother didn't speak to me for nearly a year after that. And only then, it was to tell me that my sister had committed suicide at the camp."

I looked into his eyes again and saw what I had been fearing. Recognition.

"You said something about a walk?" I asked and stood, pushing away the guilt the memories had evoked.

Of course, we walked directly to the lake. I knew now that this was a place we shared and felt a momentary pang at the lost memories.

I sat down in the shade as the day had become warm, and it would mean a little less visibility. From what was said earlier, I had a feeling Jensen was trying to tell me I was under surveillance.

"She's not dead, is she?" I asked.

Without answering he looked at me, touched his ear and made a circling motion with his finger. I frowned at him. I understood he was telling me that the trees had ears, but what did it matter. Obviously, everyone knew the answer except me.

Sensing my irritation, he stood and began unbuttoning his shirt. He kicked off his boots as he pulled the dark shirt off, then moved to his belt.

I was mesmerized. The movements were swift and efficient. A memory flashed through my brain of a similar experience, except it was much slower, and laughter filled the air. A feeling of seclusion and lack of worry made my chest ache for something I wasn't even sure was real.

He left his cotton underwear on and stepped into the water while stretching, then dove in. He popped up several yards away and looked back at me, then disappeared beneath the surface again. When he didn't resurface, I had an idea of where he was going.

I sat there for a moment longer, waiting to hear footsteps, or for anyone to call out. When none came, I stood and stretched. The warmth of the morning sun felt good. In preparation for the walk I'd put on a flexible pair of shorts that hugged my body. A black tank hugged my chest as well. I toed off my own boots and pulled off my shorts, stripping to the small thong I wore underneath. They were the most comfortable when running and moving, as I didn't have to worry about them riding up.

I folded our clothes and set them next to a tree. Turning back to the small lake, I ran full force and dove into the water. The water nearly knocked the breath out of me, it was so cold. I surfaced near the same place Jensen had, then dove under again and swam under the water to the waterfall.

I surfaced again on the other side of the gentle roaring. Jensen stood in the cave entrance and held out a hand. I took it without hesitation and he lifted me up out of the water as if I weighed nothing.

I shivered, but not because of the temperature. My stomach clenched and my thighs shook. My feet hit solid ground and I had the nearly impossible urge to place my hands on his chest and rise to my toes so I could lay my lips on his. I looked into his eyes and they seemed to mirror my instincts, which made it even harder to turn away and walk past him into the cavern.

I heard his deep sigh and felt exactly the same, but I couldn't be rash until I knew what the hell was going on. The last thing that I would allow was someone to manipulate me. Jensen followed me with the lantern. I waited until we found the pools at the end of the cavern before asking again.

"She's not dead, is she?" I repeated, breathing deeply the warm humid air around me.

"Why do you ask that?"

"Because I heard her voice last night, I think, talking about me with Daily. And there was such hatred and bitterness in it. Which would make sense, considering she may have been forced into the doctor role she had loathed here." The pain was fresh and painful as it hit me anew. I knuckled a tear from my cheek and pushed away Jensen's hand as he tried to comfort me. "No, she should be. I completely screwed up her life."

Her whisky colored eyes filled with anger from that first day I arrived at the camp flashed through my thoughts. I sat by a pool and stuck my feet in to warm them.

"Hell, I'm pretty sure I've screwed up a lot of people's

lives, including my own."

Jensen sat patiently next to me as I pushed away the pain. There was nothing that I could do about it. The choice had been made, by me, and now I had to live with the consequences. I began to wonder if I had ever expected to come back.

I noted how different Jensen was from Daily. Quiet, guarded, brooding.

"Did I ruin yours?" I asked suddenly.

"Well..." Jensen cleared his throat. "That is a loaded question if I've ever heard one."

"Yes," I nodded. "But you seem to be the only one giving me straight answers."

Jensen frowned and moved his feet in the water.

"No," he let out a breath that he seemed to have been holding and turned to look at me. "No you didn't. I told myself you did for a long time."

Jensen chuckled mirthlessly and leaned back, studying the cave ceiling and moving his feet lazily next to mine. I let him take his time. It slowly dawned on me that this might have been the first time he'd spoken about it to anyone.

"When you told me that you were going back to finish your career, in order to become a sleeper for the Resistance, I fought you. I fought you every step of the way. I told you all the reasons why it should be someone else. I listed all the risks. I begged. I pleaded. We fought for weeks before you underwent the surgery. You left me a letter..."

Jensen choked and cleared his throat, then laughed it off. I stayed silent, listening to the pain as he remembered those last days. He must have loved me to hold this much pain in a memory. I had the urge to touch him, but I held back. Now was not the time.

"You left me a letter," he continued, his voice stronger and more dispassionate. The way I used to recite field reports. "I came back from a survey mission, which had been an odd order because I didn't usually do field missions. At the time I had been the only medic with formal training on site.

"I came home to our cabin that we'd built together and found it on the table. Tossed there like an afterthought. I knew something was wrong, but I ignored the letter at first. I didn't want to open it, so I waited. I unpacked my go-bag, I cleaned up and I sat at the table, staring at that letter for I don't know how long. I think hours?"

Jensen seemed to ask the question as if I knew the answer, though I knew it was rhetorical.

"When I opened the letter, I still couldn't read it. I held it in my hands as the words seemed to melt off the page. Certain ones popped out at me so I got the gist before I crumpled it up and threw it across the room.

"Sorry, I love you, Forget me, it's for the greater good, Always Yours," those last words stuck in his throat and he leaned forward into the warm pool, letting himself slip in and under.

When he surfaced, he laughed and moved to the other side, as far away as the pool let him get from me.

"It turned out that you'd recruited someone from the Reformation Camp to your cause to erase your memory. The hold up before was because I refused to do it. So you went around me and found someone else to mess with your brain. Classic Cas."

The name he called me triggered something and my head began to split open. Flashes of memory poured in like scalding water. My chest ached and my eyes burned as the onslaught of feelings cascaded into me, stormy ocean waters breaking on the sand.

"Why don't you get your husband to do it?" Daily scoffed, his voice filled with bitterness.

"Because he can't be what I need right now," I responded.

We hurried through the dark familiar forests toward the camp.

"He can't?" I heard the small hope in his voice and fanned the flame.

"I know you'll protect me, Daily," I told him. "And I can't trust him the way I trust you."

A small lie to make sure he did as told.

"You will be my handler," I told him. "You will help me stay embedded. No one knows you in the cities. You've grown up in the mountains, completely undetected. That is uniquely useful for our cause."

I stopped in my tracks and he bumped into me as I turned.

"Can I count on you to do everything necessary to make sure my mission succeeds?"

"You can count on me Sir!" Daily performed a quick salute.

"Good," I nodded as we continued. "I need to record a few things so that if something goes wrong, I can remind myself of what's true, or what needs to be true in the moment to get me to do my job."

"Yes, Sir," Daily followed close behind me.

"Then I'm going in for surgery," I told him. "You will watch the entire procedure and listen to the doctor tell you how to trigger my status, or put me back to sleep. Do you understand?"

"Sir, Yes, Sir!"

My own voice faded as I blinked my eyes open.

"Casandra," Jensen was holding my head in his wet lap. "Casandra, can you stand?"

"I..." I cleared my throat. "Yeah."

I struggled as my head felt like it was full of cotton.

"What did you see?" He asked me as he helped me to my feet.

"It wasn't what I saw, more what I felt," I told him. "I think I was on the way to write the letter to you and record some video messages to myself."

I frowned as what I said in the memory sank in. I'd viewed one of those messages and now I'm wondering if it was one of the 'true in the moment' videos. And what happened to the rest of them?

"Your nose is bleeding," Jensen put my arm around his

shoulders but he didn't attempt to pick me up, like he had in the memory with the wolf.

"What happened to Aurora?" I asked as I wiped at my nose.

He hesitated for a moment before answering, "She died."

"I'm sorry," I replied blankly.

"So am I," Jensen supported my weight as we walked through the cave and toward the roaring water of the falls.

We slipped into the water and swam to shore in silence. More of the pieces were falling into place. I had more questions than ever and now I wanted to be alone to chew on them. At the same time, I didn't want Jensen to leave. There seemed to be an invisible cord connecting us and now I was just starting to feel the gentle tugs again.

"So what did you feel?" Jensen grabbed the towel he'd left and I sat on mine.

"I felt..." I tried to interpret the pain. "Heartache. Deep soul wrenching heartache. I felt guilt, but more than that I felt a vocation. I knew in the moment, with a righteousness, that this was the right thing to do."

"Ah..." Jensen leaned against a nearby rock.

"But..."

"But?" He cleaned the water out of his ear as I thought.

"But I don't know why I felt that way," I told him. "And I'm wondering if I was a liar."

"A liar?" Jensen frowned. "You were a lot of things, but a liar was never one of them."

"Well my memory was of manipulating someone I knew liked me," I confessed. "And I wonder if because of that I ruined any possible future for us. I'm also wondering if I did it on purpose."

"There has to be more to it," Jensen shrugged and I laughed weakly, ending on a cough.

"You have that much faith in me, that you'd blindly defend me?"

"Yes," Jensen stood and offered a hand to help me up.

The simple answer had the heartache back in full force and I again questioned who I was. Did I deserve that kind of loyalty? I stared at his hand before taking the offer. Again in silence we walked back to the barracks and headed to the showers. There was only one set of operating showers, so it was open to all sexes. As I undressed, a flash of the memory that I'd dreamed filtered in and I felt a low tug in my belly.

I peeked over my shoulder as I saw he'd already undressed and was showering. I could feel his hands on me and I knew what it was to have him inside of me. He looked over his shoulder and I looked away as I finished stripping. I kicked away the clothing and walked to the metal heads protruding through the walls. I pressed the button, which I knew would give me three minutes of water.

It was chow time, so all the other showers were empty as the soldiers off duty grabbed food. I kept my back to where Jensen stood and washed mechanically. The sight of his tall, broad and muscled body drifted back to me and I shook it away.

"Cas," a whisper came from behind me and a thrill went up my spine as I recognized it.

He didn't touch me, but he stood close enough that I could feel the warmth of his body and I instinctively leaned backward. When his naked body came into contact with mine, it was like our restraints broke. I reached back and circled his neck with my arm and tilted my head to give him better access to my neck.

I felt his teeth scrape against my neck as one arm circled my waist and pulled me more firmly against him. I sucked in air as pain bloomed from the pressure on my wound, but it quickly turned into a deep moan as his free hand grazed my nipple which was already hard and taut.

I felt his hardness press against my back and rub against me. I pushed back, torturing us both. I turned and saw his eyes clouded with a lust I mirrored. I circled both my arms around his neck and pulled him to me so that his weight pinned me to the wall. His hands were everywhere and I moved with him when they moved to my hips. He lifted me up and I grabbed the metal faucet for leverage.

Nearly blind with need, he pushed slowly against me as I opened for him. My hips moved toward him in a silent plea, but he held my hips steady until I looked at him.

"Are you sure?" He asked me, his eyes nearly begging me not to stop him. But he was still taking the time to ask and I melted. I could end this if I wanted. I could walk away.

I moved my hips and he slid in just a little more.

"I need you to say it," his voice was strained. "Please."

I watched and reveled in his restraint, wondering what it would be like if he let go. I smiled down at him.

"I'm sure," I said, and that was all it took.

Suddenly he was in me, and we both groaned with the sensation.

"Oh, Goddess," I moaned and let go of the faucet to pull his face to mine.

Our tongues mingled as he moved slowly, so slowly I thought that I would burst. It built in me like a steady stream until I came. As soon as I did he was like a jackhammer, building it up all over again.

I tried to keep up but I had no leverage. I was helpless to the onslaught of pleasure. As I neared the edge again I opened my eyes and saw that he was watching me intently.

"Come with me," I told him, and together we flew over the edge.

 The faucet dripped lazily on the back of his neck as it ended and I wondered how that could have possibly been only three minutes, or maybe I just didn't notice when the water turned off.

It had felt like a lifetime and one second all at once. I remained in a contented haze that felt familiar and heartbreaking at the same time. I knew we should move, but I didn't want to shatter the bubble of heaven we'd created. In this moment we could be anyone and no one. No duties, no responsibilities, no Resistance.

When he began to shake, I felt an overpowering urge to comfort him. With me in his arms he slowly lowered to the ground, quaking and cradling me in his lap. I kept him close and let him lean in.

"It's ok," I murmured, running my hand through his wet hair. "You're safe."

When he leaned back I expected a ravaged face. An inkling of the small heartache I felt. But instead, I stared stunned at the eyes which laughed back at me. The sight of my confusion pushed him even farther and he began to howl with laughter. I started to stand, but he pulled me back onto his lap and held me there until his laughter subsided.

I sat, feeling a wave of humiliation wash over me.

"What's so funny?" I gritted out between my clenched teeth.

"Us," his eyes were serious now when I looked back. The mirth had vanished.

"What about it?" I demanded. "I know I'm a little rusty, but I thought it was pretty good."

"That's not what I'm laughing about," a smile stretched lightly across his face but didn't quite reach his eyes.

"We should go, someone could come in any minute," I tried to stand but he just tugged me back down again. Instead of allowing it this time I rolled with the tug and had him pinned on the ground within seconds. "I said, we need to get up."

The same spark of humor ignited in his eyes again as he held his hands up in a form of truce. I nodded and began to get up. Fast as lightning, he moved in on my unsteady stance and kicked my feet out from under me. He caught me before I could bang my head on the tile, but the pressure of his body on mine lit the fire I thought had gone dormant.

"We can go in a minute," Jensen said. "It won't be the end of the world for anyone to see us together."

I thought about that for a moment and realized he was right. I shouldn't be afraid of being discovered with someone. I shouldn't be afraid of ruining the reputation of the leader of the Resistance, since I wasn't completely sold on the measures we'd taken so far.

"Relax," Jensen rolled to reverse our positions.

I now lay sprawled over his chest, looking down at him as my wet hair slapped the side of his face. He grinned up at me. Memories trickled in and planted themselves in my brain, seeds starting to grow. Small things, tiny loving gestures from him after he rescued me that one day. Finding each other in the water. Discovering the caves. The first time we made love, and how incredibly nervous I was. While I hadn't been a virgin, it was the first time I'd been with someone whom I cared deeply for.

The memories of the blooming of our love had my face falling and my eyes burning. I'd thrown that away. I'd looked at him and told him that the mission was more important than he was. By all accounts, I should have died. Why hadn't I? Did I owe Daily my life? Is that why I'm still here? I never should have been brought back. As the old anxieties began to sink in, I pushed them away for just a minute to drown in the eyes I'd now had the pleasure of falling in love with twice.

"Jen," I whispered, and his face split from ear to ear.

"Cas," he hugged me tightly and I did my best to get closer. "You remember me."

"I do," I sighed as I let myself drift for just a moment.

"If I'd known that this would make you remember me, maybe I would have ravaged you the first day you came back."

"Maybe," I chuckled. "But we all know you would've lost that fight."

"Maybe," we stayed like that for a moment longer until the sound of an opening and closing exterior door had me scrambling up and starting a shower again.

Jensen laughed and rose himself to finish the cleaning we'd originally planned. Though we occupied separate areas of the shower and people were now joining us, I continued to sneak peeks at Jensen.

My Jen, I'd called him before.

How could I have possibly forgotten him?

We finished in a rush and headed back to the cabin. I walked in and threw my extra clothes in the nearest clothing bin. I was about to turn and say something to Jensen, when I saw the look on his face.

Immediately I was on guard, and turned to face the threat.

Daily sat at the kitchen table. I frowned at him, but instinctively relaxed my stance.

"What are you doing here Daily?" I wondered, not moving any closer.

"Well I've been waiting here for a couple of hours so we could talk about your options," he stated gruffly as he looked past me to Jensen.

"Options?" Jensen stepped forward then, but I put a hand up and he halted in his tracks.

"Options?" I repeated his words.

"Well," Daily had the courtesy to look embarrassed. "To recover your memory without any side-effects, like the headaches, bloody noses and the like."

"I didn't realize I had options," I told him, smiling as if he were being sweet and he ate it up, relaxing into his chair. "I thought any further procedure could result in my death."

I walked forward calmly and sat down next to him,

setting my elbows on the table and leaning toward him, as if I were hanging on his next words. Jensen, confused but cautious, sat across from him on my other side. I realized now that he knew me well enough that a change this dramatic in my demeanor meant to play along. I'd need to tell him everything I suspected later.

Daily sat preening next to me, and happily mimicked my posture by leaning in as well.

"Did you remember something?" Daily was eager to hear that I'd remembered him, and I did. Just not in the way he wanted me to.

"I did," I smiled wide and gave him a wink. A genuine happiness seemed to bloom in him that almost made me regret my current deception.

Almost.

He began to lean forward even more, almost as if to kiss me, and I swept my hair forward.

"I need to find my brush," I swept it back over my head and stood quickly, moving to rummage through my drawers. "Go ahead and talk about my options, Lover."

The word almost stuck in my throat, so I threw my hair over my face to brush it forward. It gave my face a curtain as I sat on a couch across the room from the two at the table. Daily didn't speak immediately but stared at Jensen, who suddenly found something very interesting outside the window.

"Where were you two?" Daily asked suddenly, and I wondered if I'd blown it by dodging the kiss. The idea of his lips on mine after what I'd just shared with Jen made me want to vomit.

"We went for a short hike, then a swim to cool off," I told him, which he could easily verify. "Then we went and showered off. Why?"

I let my hair part so I could make eye contact with Daily, and raised a brow before resuming my personal grooming.

"I was just wondering," he shrugged it off. "Now that you remember, maybe you don't need the other options."

"But I don't have the rest of my memories," I stated as I pulled my hair back and into a small knot at the nape of my neck. "Like what happened right before I came here."

I watched his face for any indication of if he knew what I was talking about but all I saw was a stone wall. Which meant he did.

"I told you what happened," Daily reminded me.

"Of course you did," I smiled at him. "But you know I hate relying on intel, I'd much rather scope something out myself, right?"

I stood and walked forward slowly, keeping my eyes on his as I walked toward Daily. I moved my hips a bit more than normal. I saw from the corner of my eyes that Jensen's hands were clenched under the table, but I couldn't let that stop me. Daily sat, feet flat, legs apart. I set the brush on the table when I reached him and sat on his lap. I weaved my hands behind his neck and through his hair, smiling lightly. I let my eyes go blank and pretended it was Jensen. I lifted my legs and through them over the arm of the chair so that all of my weight was on him.

When I made eye contact with him his ice blue eyes twinkled as they switched from me to Jensen. He was taking a deep pleasure in Jensen's discomfort. To draw his attention fully to me, I laid my lips on his. Without waiting a beat, his tongue was thrusting into my mouth and I nearly gagged. His hands grabbed my ass and rubbed me against his hardening crotch. I knew I was putting myself at risk, but I couldn't see any other way forward. I participated as much as I dared, before extricating myself from his hold. Which was no easy task.

"Daily," I chided lightly and slapped his hands away as he tried to pull me onto his lap again and sat in the chair next to him. "We have company."

"He could leave," Daily moved to pull me forward again.

"Just be patient," I smiled as a splitting headache ripped through my skull for a second, then it was gone.

Something here.

"Uh Oh," I wiped at the nose that had started to bleed. "You'd better hurry up with those options." I sent up a silent thanks to whoever was watching over me, and stood to grab something to staunch it.

"Well," Daily started. "We could do something like a reverse procedure."

"Reverse?" Jensen asked, incredulous.

"Yeah," Daily responded. "We would go in..."

"Who's 'we'?" I asked from the small bathroom. I looked in the mirror and cleaned my face as much as possible then stuck some paper in my nose and waited for the bleeding to stop.

"Uh..." I could almost hear the eye contact between him and Jen. "The head doctor and their team."

"I thought Jensen was head of medical," I stated.

"He was," Daily seemed to scoff a bit. "Until you appointed someone more deserving of the position."

"Huh," I, of course, had no memory of appointing anyone else, but Jensen wasn't contradicting him. "So what's a reverse procedure, exactly?"

"Well, it's like when they build the bridges over your memory cores with Redaction," he said. "Only a reverse redaction is like burning those bridges."

"And that will retrieve all of my lost memories?" I asked as I inserted another paper into my nose. The bleeding was taking a long time to stop.

"Most of them," he confirmed.

"What are the risks?" Jensen asked.

"What do you mean?" Daily returned, as if annoyed at the question. "The same as a normal procedure."

"The same?" Jensen seemed to be annoyed right back. "That hardly seems possible when this wouldn't be her first time getting cut open. In fact, it would be more likely that it would be extremely dangerous. What happens if she doesn't have the procedure?"

I sifted through the contents of the cupboards under the sink and came up with a small eye liner pencil. Using toilet paper, I wrote down everything that I knew and had remembered. It was a long list and almost none of the pieces connected. I was missing something big and I felt like it was right in front of me. I rolled up the paper, put the pencil away and stepped to the doorway of the tiny bathroom.

I listened to them argue back and forth for a while leaning against the doorway, and without much preamble, let myself fall out of the entry and hit the floor hard. I kept my eyes shut as they both ran to me, arguing still. Jensen rolled me over and shined his damn penlight in my eyes. He narrowed his eyes, but swore.

"Go get help," he barked at Daily. "She's hemorrhaging."

Daily was out the door in a flash and I let my eyes focus on Jensen as he frowned at me.

"What the hell was that all about?"

I frowned back at him, shook my head and reached up to the hand that held my cheek, pushing the paper into his other hand. His brows raised quizzically, but that was all the time we had before Daily ran back in with a bunch of grunts. They threw me onto a stretcher and marched me out the door quickly. I continued to keep my eyes closed, leaving my arms limp and dangling. I knew now that the only person I could trust here was Jensen.

At least I wasn't completely alone.

Though I couldn't see, I was listening to everything around me. Every breath, every voice.

I concentrated on my heart beat. I breathed in a shallow breath every 25 seconds and released a puff of air every 5 seconds, until it was time to take another shallow breath. If my eyes hadn't been closed already I would have unfocused them so they appeared glassy. I did keep one eye cracked slightly. Not so that I could see what was going on around me, but so that my pupils would react differently when they pulled them open.

As I thought, someone ripped open one eyelid and shone a light in it, then the other.

"Pupils unequal, but responsive," a voice noted as I felt the warm air on my skin as we moved.

A pressure on my bicep told me they were taking my blood pressure. I concentrated again on my breathing and heartbeat, letting everything else fall away. I kept myself awake by digging one of my nails into the palm of my hand.

"BP dropping rapidly and she's bradycardic," another voice noted.

"We're losing her!" Daily yelled. "Do something."

The panicked whine in his voice would have been comical in any other circumstance.

The air changed and the ground became stable, but we continued to move as we entered the medical hall. I could hear the squeaking wheels of the gurney as they rushed me toward the operating room.

"What happened?" A familiar voice demanded.

"Do something," Daily repeated, this time with a desperate whinge in his voice.

"I'll do what I can," the voice sighed as I rolled to a stop, as if exasperated. "But we knew this could be an outcome."

"Just fix her!"

The clanking of medical tools sounded next to me, then came the squeak of another set of wheels which I'd been hoping for. As they hooked up my finger to find my pulse and I listened to it flatline, pump once, then flatline again.

"Asystole!" Someone cried.

"Charge to three-hundred," the familiar voice became grumpy. "Get him out of here."

I heard a struggle and let myself float near unconsciousness.

"Clear!"

At that moment I took a deep breath and opened my eyes, knocking the paddles out of her hands.

A shocked gasp moved through the room as I took one of

the paddles and pressed it to my sister's neck.

"You have some explaining to do, *Chase*," I told her.

My sister was alive and she had the gall to grin.

I stared into the whiskey eyes that used to be warm but were now shrouded in ice.

I didn't see fear as she sized me up, but more of an annoyance.

"I'm surprised you aren't seizing," Chase smirked. "Usually when you remember you're on the floor, slobbering all over yourself."

I kept my gaze steady and watched her eyes narrow.

"You haven't remembered," she said, low enough that only I could hear, then raised her voice to the rest of the room. "Everyone out."

"But," Daily began.

"I said out!"

"Yes, sir!" Came the reply from the eight people that had wheeled me into the surgery room. I didn't bother to look to see if Daily was still there.

"Jen!" I called, and heard the door swing open and closed.

"I'm here," came his soft response. "The room is empty."

"Good," I dropped the paddle and punched my sister in the nose.

Swearing she stumbled backward, overturning the table of medical supplies before slamming into the wall. Her beautiful blonde hair was cropped short like everyone else. She had always been thin and gangly, so if it weren't for her eyes I wouldn't have known for sure it was her. Chase fit right in with the androgyny of the Resistance.

"Watch the door," I called over my shoulder to Jensen. "Don't let anyone else in here. I need answers."

"How did you know they would bring you to me?" Chase wiped the back of her hand through the blood weeping from her nose, then turned and spit more onto the ground.

"I didn't," I said. "Not for sure. But the way that Daily was pushing for me to go through the procedure again made me think it might happen without my consent the next time I had an episode. So I took a risk. Worst case scenario, I'd end up with a couple of holes in my arm and get rehydrated."

"I'll remember to strap you down, next time," Chase smiled, which showed off her blood smeared teeth.

"What makes you think there will be a next time, Chastity?"

Chase grinned wider at the mention of her full name.

"No one has called me that in so long, I'd almost forgotten it had been real," she sighed. "And it's only a matter of time before you need another procedure. Your neural pathways are fried."

The sound of her amusement made my stomach roll.

"What do you mean, fried?"

"I mean, you're only really supposed to be reset four, maybe max five times before things start to break down," Chase chuckled.

"How many times have I been reset?"

"Last count?" Chase paused as she considered. "Twenty-one."

"Twenty-one times?" I repeated as my heart began to sink.

"Yup," she shrugged. "Though there's probably been unreported times. Daily was resetting you every time you remembered you didn't like him."

I could hear Jensen shuffling as he listened.

"How is that possible?" I demanded. "How could you let him do that to me?"

"It's possible because you commanded it," Chase smiled slowly, but the expression was sharp. "And I was following your orders to the letter."

"Will another procedure fix it?"

"Oh hell no," Chase laughed out right, and wiped the blood that still trickled down her nose.

"Then why would I agree?"

"Because you get just a little bit more time if you submit."

"What does that mean?" I growled.

"It means..." Chase drew out the words. "That by

bypassing the fried neural pathways, and choosing the healthy ones your brain *probably* won't melt down as fast, but it will continue to deteriorate until you can't remember five minutes ago."

"Explain exactly what 'meltdown' means."

"You want me to draw you a diagram?" Chase asked sarcastically.

"Yes," I replied.

I jumped back up on the operating table.

"You've got a pen in your pocket there," I gestured to her lab coat. "Draw me a diagram. Break it down so that I know exactly what is going on."

"I don't know why I bother," Grumbling to herself, Chase took out the pen and turned her back to me while swiping the cuff of her white coat under her nose, making red streaks.

"Think of your neural pathways as a walking trail," she began and drew a straight line on the wall. "The more normal or 'basic memory' is what I would consider a direct path."

Chase then drew a snaking line, and a zig-zagging line underneath the straight line.

"When you are bypassing a memory," Chase began.

"Why bypass?"

"Are you going to interrupt me the entire time?" She demanded.

"Probably," I shrugged unapologetically.

"Because," Chase gritted her teeth. "It's not possible to erase memories completely, similar to a circuit board. Pulling out a circuit is much more dangerous than bypassing it."

"So is it like a walking path or a circuit board?"

"I'm going to ignore you now," Chase turned back to her diagram to continue. "When you want to bypass a memory, you insert another pathway and more or less tie it off."

I could hear the echoes of this in my head, a missing dream just out of reach.

Chase drew a circle, bisecting the line and then two dots on either side, then connected them creating a half circle.

"This would be how you bypass a standard memory," Chase capped her pen and turned back.

"What exactly would a standard memory be considered," I asked.

"Non-confrontational or emotional memories."

"Like what I ate for breakfast?"

"Exactly," she nodded. "And eventually the pathway can become permanent because the brain can feel the gap and many people create their own memories to insert into the missing spot, or like a computer defragments a hard drive it just fills the space with something else."

"So it is more like circuitry?" I asked.

"When it comes to standard memories," Chase frowned. "Yes."

"So what about bypassing non-standard memories?" I asked.

"That's when you start having issues," Chase said. "And why the Uniformity uses borderline personality disorders or high functioning sociopaths for this specific procedure in intelligence gathering."

"Because they have a lower number of emotional memories?" I guessed.

"Yes," Chase smirked at me. "But when you decided to go on this suicide mission, you didn't know that. You thought you were being clever."

"How do you bypass non-standard memories?" I asked, ignoring her.

"Similar to the standard, but they require more upkeep and to stay away from something that might trigger the bypass to fail," Chase continued and drew a straight line through the snaked and zig zagged lines. "Depending on how deep the emotions are connected to the memory, it can slowly erode the bypass. Eventually, if you put the bypass in enough times, it shreds the original neural path and the bypasses last even less time. Reality becomes hard to interpret. Fires erupt in your brains as small hemorrhages begin to bleed. Soon you won't be able to retain any memories because your pathways will be unsustainable."

"What kind of a trigger?"

"I like that you ignored the last part," Chase chuckled. "For you, if we needed you brought out of your sleeper state to extract specific data, we would show you a picture of Jensen."

I heard a sharp intake of breath from behind me, but kept my focus on the stranger in front of me. She wasn't my sister anymore, that much was obvious.

"In that way, you were ideal," Chase said. "You were very easy to pull out. The hard part was putting you back under, so we experimented while you were in college."

"How long have you been here?" I asked.

"Since you went back," Chase said in a low voice, so full of malice that I was surprised. "You stole everything from me."

"What do you mean?"

An explosion of noise came from behind me and I ducked forward then turned toward the door, preparing to fight. Soldiers with guns burst into the room. Jensen ducked, but Daily was leading the charge and had a semi-automatic rifle pointed at his chest before he could react.

"I mean, you stole *everything* from me," Chase repeated. "You stuck me in this hell hole and left me to rot. I had *plans*. I had *dreams*. But you didn't care. You saw an up and coming doctor and you stole my future. Now lay down, so I can finish stealing yours."

"No," I stood back from the table.

"Do it," Daily said, his gaze not wavering from Jensen. "Or I'll put a bullet in your bitch's head."

The amount of hatred and vitriol that spewed from that statement started to make some pieces fit together, and as they did my skull seemed to catch fire. Someone screamed and screamed. Shouts rang out and bullets pinged through the room. I could feel hot breath on my neck, pressure on top of me, and someone repeating *Thank you* over and over again.

Not now, I thought.

But it was no use. I collapsed as the force of this memory ripped through my brain. My entire body hurt with the memory. Someone was raping me. *No,* I thought. Someone *had* raped me. I tried to get back up, but I was already strapped down.

My eyes flew open, and looked into the ice blue of those who had forced themselves on me.

Thank you, thank you. He'd chanted as he'd pushed himself into me over and over.

My stomach turned as the memory set new fires in my brain. I turned and wretched the contents of my stomach onto the ground.

That's when I saw the blood. I looked around the room frantically, looking for Jensen.

"Where is he?" I demanded, struggling against the bonds. "What have you done?"

"What had to be done to make you mine," Daily smiled slowly. "Since you won't be mine the way you are, I have to keep fixing you so that you remember that you love me."

"I've never loved you," I turned to Chase who was putting on gloves, already masked. "Chase don't do this. He raped me."

Chase paused and her eyes flicked to Daily, who had the gall to look sheepish.

"So that's why she was broken this last time," Chase said dully as she continued to prepare. "Don't worry, we'll make sure you forget that again."

Someone held a mask over my face and the lights around me began to dim. I struggled as much as I could, but I had no options. I had no way to fight. I was helpless. I fought for every breath, until the darkness consumed me.

I will remember, I thought. *Eventually.*

Feelings passed through me like water through a sieve. I could feel them moving, but I couldn't grasp their meaning. It was as if I lay in the sunlight with eyes closed and watched the shadow theatre behind my eyelids.

Thoughts were even harder to grasp. Sounds pressed against my ears, but failed to be processed. I drifted and wondered why something was pushing against my bubble. Time stood still or continued to pass, I wasn't sure which and it didn't seem to matter. I had nowhere and nothing to be. I wondered idly what had come before this bloom of contentment, but the passing thought hurt so I let it go. I sighed and settled in, but something wouldn't stop bothering me. It was a tiny mosquito in my perfect paradise. It would come closer and I could hear the hum, then dissipate as I waved it away.

It was nagging and out of reach. All I wanted was to continue to drift.

Cas...

Just a whisper on the wind.

Casandra...

A passing breeze, ran a chill up my spine.

"Wake up!"

The scream had me sitting forward and I slammed my head into the dash of a moving vehicle.

"Fuck!"

"You need to be awake!" Jensen yelled at me from the driver's seat as we sped down a dark forested road. Downed trees littered the sides of the path and the trees around us seemed to bow in what looked like extremely windy conditions.

"What the fuck is going on?" I demanded. I looked around and saw that I was wearing a dirty hospital gown. Then it came back. "Holy shit, how did you get to me?"

I remembered seeing blood and hearing a gunshot.

"Where are you hit?" I asked.

"Put your seatbelt on!" He yelled at me as we sped through the path, narrowly avoiding a tree as it crumpled under its own weight.

"What the hell is going on?" I pulled the belt over and noticed that my hair wasn't in the way when I moved. I reached up and felt the sheer buzz. I wasn't vain, but I did frown. I felt a bit of wet as I explored my scalp.

"Feels like you got to me just in time," I said.

"Barely," Jensen replied. "I was able to disengage the generator and without that they were out of luck. The storm that blew in was the perfect cover. I knew it was now or never to get you out."

"Are you hurt?" I asked.

"You don't have to worry about that," he tried to send me a smile, but he was concentrating on the path. "Up ahead we are going to be ditching this vehicle and taking another one I stashed a while back. One that doesn't have a tracker."

"Mmm," my eyelids were drooping.

"Cas!" He yelled and I jerked awake again.

"What?"

"I need you to stay awake," Jensen replied. "You were taken off the meds prematurely and you're running the risk of your lungs stopping. Just concentrate on your breathing and stay awake. Here put these on."

He reached into the back and threw a pair of my basic training pants and a tee. I pulled them on, as careful as I could be.

Less than a minute after I'd finished dressing, Jensen pulled the vehicle over, grabbed some bags from the back seat, then ran to my side of the car. I'd barely unbuckled when he plucked me out of the car. I thought about protesting, but I knew he'd do it anyway. He ran for what seemed like a mile and I began to wonder where we were going.

Abruptly he stopped, set me down, and threw the bags next to me. I could barely see and the wind howled around us. There was a deafening crack in the distance that said another tree was giving in to the torrent.

Jensen walked to a mound of what looked like leaves and

pulled a boned disc camouflage cover from the top of a motorcycle and sidecar.

"Are you sure that can run?" I asked.

He didn't even bother to answer as he grabbed me, gently set me in the sidecar and packed the bags around me. He took a helmet and pulled it on, then handed me another.

As I pulled it on, he started the cycle and it purred like a kitten. He spared me a glance with a raised eyebrow as he shot through the underbrush and onto an old asphalt road. The light was dim, but illuminated our surroundings well enough. I finished hooking on my helmet and pulled down the goggles to cover my eyes, which had started to leak with the air flow and whipping wind. The air changed constantly from warm to freezing and I could hear it raging around the cycle.

After only a few miles we moved to another forestry road that ended quickly at a log-walled community.

Jensen shut off the engine and waited.

"Hallo?" A gravelly voice called from the other side of the wall.

"Heiligtum!" Jensen responded.

The doors immediately swung open and Jensen pushed the cycle off to the side before gathering the bags and then me.

There was a short heated exchange in what sounded like German as Jensen walked through the gates and then they were shut behind us. The word that Jensen had shouted at the other side of the door was muttered here and there. Candles were being lit and people were peeking out of cabins. We were led to a larger cabin and the door swung open. Another man had a second heated exchange with the one that had let us in, but no one was looking at Jensen or I. The second man, clad in a pair of black trousers, a button up white shirt and suspenders that hung from his waist, sighed grievously then turned abruptly.

Jensen took that to mean he was to follow. He led us to a small room off the main area that looked like a study. He gestured to the small sofa where Jensen laid me down. The man that had led us there kept his back to Jensen.

"I have to leave," Jensen told me.

"What?" I gaped at him. "No you can't."

"I can't stay here," he gasped as he grabbed his side.

I saw a concerned twitch from the man in the doorway, but he never said anything or even turned.

"You need to rest," I told him. "You're hurt."

"I can't stay," Jensen moved past the man by the door but only made it a few feet before he collapsed.

"Scheisse," the man grumbled and moved toward Jensen. He called to the man in the doorway and they both disappeared upstairs with him.

I could hear yelling from upstairs, but I was so tired I couldn't get up to investigate. I wanted to know where the hell we were, but I couldn't bring myself to try and piece it together. I knew I was supposed to be doing something, but everything quickly faded away and soon I was drifting again.

I drifted in a dark void. I floated in waves of cold and warmth. I heard voices that were like soothing screeches and the waves felt like soft metal. Everything inside of me was coming apart at the seams, yet seemed to be made of concrete.

My eyes flew open and I jumped from a bed. A child stood inches from me as I reached for the weapon that no longer resided on my hip. It took a moment before thoughts and memories began crashing into one another. A jumble of confusion and revelation. My head screeched to a stop and I focused again on the child who sat on the floor, looking up at me in wonder.

After a moment of staring at each other, the child broke into a grin. Short cropped blond hair framed his face. He looked to be about twelve.

"Hallo," he said after a moment.

"Hi," I smiled unsure. "Uh, do you know where my friend is?"

It was his turn to look confused and I remembered they

seemed to speak a different language here. I tried to bring back the words I'd heard.

"Uh," I tried to bring back the rudimentary knowledge I had of the language. I had always thought that when you always had a translator on you, it was pointless to learn a new language. Obviously I was wrong. "Sprechen sie Deutsch?"

"Ja!" He prattled on quickly and I lost most of it trying to translate. The words that I did catch were something akin to German.

"Wo ist mein Freund?" I repeated my earlier question the best I knew how.

"Ah, upstairs," he said in German and pointed toward the ceiling.

I moved to the door and the child skipped along behind. I heard yelling from above, so I hurried my step. I took the stairs two at a time and found Jensen, chest bandaged and unconscious in a large log bed. There were two men shouting over him in German and I couldn't even make out half of it, but one word kept repeating, 'gemieden'.

I remembered some history about the communes that the Protectorate allowed to operate as sovereign nations. If someone left the commune for the outside world, they were considered 'gemieden', or shunned.

Jensen was from here? That was an odd thought. I tried to string some words together. They seemed to be fighting over whether or not they should throw him out, and it seemed that they were leaning toward letting him stay. I wished desperately for a translator.

Right then, without opening his eyes, Jensen responded to the two men. They abruptly left the room. The boy stayed by my side and began talking excitedly at Jensen.

I walked forward and took his hand, sitting on the bed next to him. He peaked an eye open and sent me a wan smile.

"How are you, gorgeous?"

"I think I'm ok, you don't look so good though," I returned.

"I feel worse," he replied.

"What's going on?" I asked. "Where are we?"

"We are at my old family home," he said. "I left to do some research about The Scourge, but because I wasn't living here, I was shunned."

"I gathered some of that," I confirmed. "How come you never told me?"

"You never asked," his smile wobbled a little.

"I didn't?" I frowned. "Not that my memory is without holes still, but I'll accept that I'm selfish enough to be that awful."

"We didn't have a lot of time together..."

"You don't need to defend me, to me," I chuckled darkly. "It's not necessary. Are we going to need to leave soon?"

"No," it was his turn to chuckle. "A loophole in the shunning."

"Loophole?" I repeated.

"Yes," he struggled for a moment to sit up and then just let himself lay back again. "Some people are more fundamental than others. My family is more centrist than the community would like, but they still follow the laws. One of the laws is that they cannot abandon anyone to die."

"Why did they leave earlier?"

"My father will address me, but many in the community won't even talk or look at me."

"So if you speak, they leave, otherwise they would be considered conversing with you?" I let out a laugh. "Well that is quite a loophole."

"It'll buy us some time," Jensen tried to shrug and grimaced.

I looked down at the boy, who was following our conversation intently.

"Is this your brother?"

"Yes," Jensen smiled at him. "He's seven."

"What?" I gaped and looked at the child I'd thought was at least twelve. "How? He looks much older than that."

"You're used to male children born outside the communes," Jensen smiled. "They develop slower and are more lean."

"Because of The Scourge?" I asked. "You said you left to study it, what did you find?"

"I got a bit distracted," Jensen squeezed my hand and I realized I must have been the distraction. "But what I was able to find out was that something didn't add up. I can't prove it yet, but I think The Scourge was manufactured by the Uniformity."

"What?" My jaw dropped. "But you don't have proof?"

"No," he sighed. "But I was getting close when the Resistance found me. Us. Come here."

"I don't want to hurt you," I tried to pull away, but he pulled me back with surprising strength.

"You won't."

I gently lay on the bed next to him, cuddled to his side and mulling over all the information.

"Did you tell me this before?" I asked.

"Yes."

"And that's why I went undercover, isn't it?"

"Yes."

It was my turn to sigh.

"We need to get to the bottom of this, but we need to find another way," I stated.

He nodded quietly before beginning to snore lightly.

I lie awake, thinking of what was happening around me and what I needed to do. There was too much to do on my own. I looked at Jensen as he slept and wondered whether or not he was strong enough.

He would be, I told myself. *He had to be.*

****

Uniformity Hierarchy

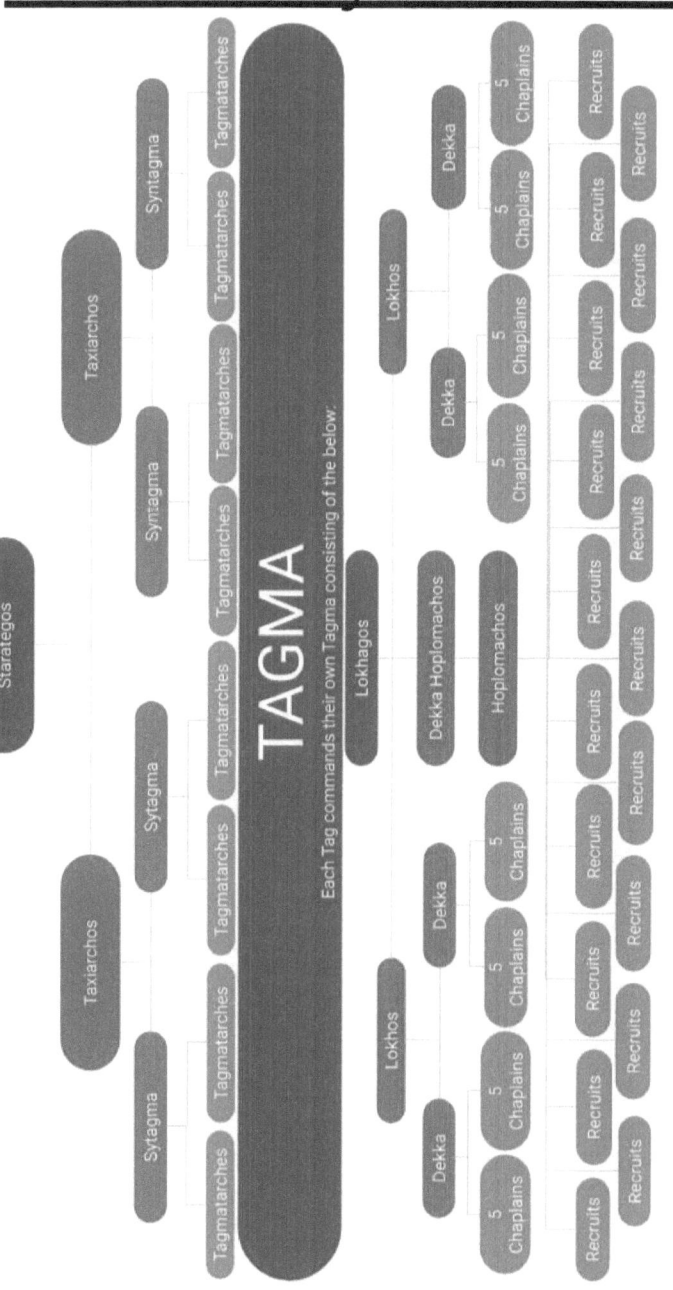

HISTORIA

2600 BCE — Dawn of Recorded Historia

2400 BCE — 1st recorded Female Leader; Kubaba

325 CE — Council of Nicaea, made up of men, determined the fate of a popular religious text. They burned any of their own ancient texts that contradicted their determinations.

508 CE — Democracy is born. Women are not allowed to vote

1096 CE — The Crusades: Nearly 200 years of religious zealotry, on behalf of the popular religious text, resulting in 1.7 million deaths.

1478 CE — The Spanish Inquisition and European witch trials. The legal persecution and torture lasted nearly 400 years, resulting in thousands dead.

1492 CE — A new continent was invaded by Spain and the systematic genocide of the indigenous people began

1692 CE — Salem witch trials in the colonies of Europe before their independence

1738 CE — Evangelicalism is born: A platform to sell salvation to the masses by defrauding and bilking its believers

1776 CE — Largest land mass Declaration for Independence: United States of America

1817 CE — Creation of the Stock Market in the United States of America

1881 CE — Women first get the right to vote, ironically, on the Isle of Man.

1914 CE — The first global war for territory. It lasted for four years and resulted in 20 million deaths.

1920 CE — Women won the right to vote in the USA.

1921 CE — The Burning of Black Wallstreet: White men, jealous of the African American prosperity in Tulsa, OK, USA, bombed the town and gutted the entirety of businesses located there. 35 square city blocks were destroyed by private aircraft.

1928 CE — Women won the right to vote in Europe.

1929 CE — U.S. stock market crash resulting in the greatest economic depression resulting in 7 million deaths

1933 CE — Protections created to prevent another economic collapse.

1938 CE — Nuclear fusion was invented

1939 CE — Second global war begins with the systematic genocide of the Jewish people in Europe.

1941 CE — Mass torture, genetic experimentation, persecution in the name of a "master race" resulting in 6 million deaths over five years

1945 CE — Second global war ended by the nuclear bombing of a small island nation resulting in more than 200,000 deaths in one day.

1965 CE — Though citizens of African decent in the USA were ratified to vote in 1865, there were suppressive tactics used by white supremacists to keep them from voting until The Voting Rights Act was passed.

1999 CE — The protections created in 1933 are repealed

*BCE – Before Common Era *CE – Common Era *UE – Uniform Era

2020 CE	2019 CE	2016 CE	2015 CE	2012 CE	2008 CE

A Global Pandemic spreads like wild-fire, where the Despot is slow to react. Using the fear and resulting deaths, he is re-elected by voter suppression and fraud

Due to global warming, the entire continent of Australia burned for months. A virus begins to spread in China.

Despot Elected through persecution of minorities and waving a popular religious text. It is irrelevant to the text's worshipers that he does not follow their tenants, only that they are validated in their beliefs.

The bid for the next President: A Despot is Born. Using Evangelism the flames of racial hatred and economic instability are fanned for a bid to power

African American President elected for second term though racial tensions are beginning to boil

Largest Stock Market Crash since 1929 & the first African American President Elected in the USA

2021 CE	2022 CE	2023 CE	2024 CE	2025 CE

After 529 years of systemic genocide, the Indigenous American population is functionally extinct. Only 6 million people exist compared to the original 60 million before the colonization of the Americas. Their population continues to dwindle, hit hard by the virus.

An assassination attempt on the Despot's life leads to the USA government demanding all civilians turn in their guns.

The USA falls into civil war: ignited by

Mass public executions of USA resistance cells.

Martial Law is declared, but unenforceable as states begin The Great Secession begins.

This has a domino effect on the World's Economy

As the smaller states in the USA cannot survive on their own, some accept reinforcements from other countries in exchange for their sovereignty.

Texas becomes its own Country. California, Oregon, and Washington form a new union called Cascadia.

Infighting over the new territories starts World War 3. The Despot declares himself ruler of the North American Divided Nations.

Still no cure for the Pandemic has been found.

2029 CE	2028 CE	2027 CE	2026 CE

Activists are still able to broadcast in the dark, hacking channels and covering the reality of the world's quick descent into fascism. There are reports of "baby farms" and "rape clinics". Abortion is globally banned, as well as any autonomy for women. Genetic experimentation runs unchecked as a search for a cure is prioritized.

Countries across the world shut down their international connective online networks to control the media and spread of information; creating a new intranet.

The Despot contracts the virus and dies, slowly, publicly. Despite being surrounded by the top doctors. His failed liver, heart and lung diseases contribute to a very quick demise.

The power vacuum consumes the world as men die in droves globally. Countries begin a systematic withdrawal from the United Nations and trade agreements

The Virus mutates and attaches itself to the Y chromosome: This mutation is later termed The Scourge

*BcE – Before Common Era *CE – Common Era *UE – Uniform Era

2030 CE

Bolstered by leaked information and government crackdown, resistance groups begin systematic revolutions. They successfully restore the international online presence by publicizing their liberation of forced birth camps.

Once one country is liberated, the groups move to another and another until.

GLOBAL UNIFORMITY

2031 CE

4 billion people perish in the aftermath of The Scourge. Men from the disease, women from mass genetic experimentation and failed back alley procedures. A vaccine is finally discovered and is administered at birth and while it keeps male children from dying, their development will never be the same.

2032 CE

International trading begins again as countries attempt to rebuild with the new vaccine.

2050 UE

It was discovered in a small sub-section of the population that were isolated before, during and after the virus was being transmitted, had recovered fully from the Scourge. So a pact was made with these small colonies that if they did not resist, and complied with the Uniformity on some provisions, they would be left to govern themselves as they saw fit.

2040 UE

The Creation of the Uniformity. Using the cure as leverage a new accord was struck and a global council of women was created. As this was the beginning of a new Era, they created a time concept to track it and begin the process to move the world forward past the tragedies together. They knew that together was better than apart and that they would be able to avoid infighting or jealousies if their global laws were of complete equity

2033 CE

With the collapse of the modern infrastructure a tentative peace was struck to help the world rebuild.

Dear Reader,

Since I was young I've struggled with depression, anxiety, and self-worth. Know that you are not alone and that you are worth everything. Fight every day and find people who will help you fight. It's ok to ask for help. Your bravery in your daily battle should not go unheard.

If you are thinking about self-harm, suicide or are worried about a loved one: Please speak out. Talk to them and encourage them to find help.

Call this number 24/7 if you are experiencing thoughts of suicide:

1(800)273-8255

I know it's hard, but you can do it. I believe in you.

#FightTheVoid

S.M. Winter

Domestic Abuse hotline: 1(800)799-SAFE(7233)
Nation Sex Assault Telephone Hotline: 1(800)656- HOPE(4673)

Other Books By S.M. Winter

True North: Book One of the Elemental Series

South of Redemption: Book Two of the Elemental Series

Western Affliction: Book Three of the Elemental Series

Coming Soon:

At Scales Edge: Part Two

Memoirs of a Time Warden

Book Four of the Elemental Series: Title TBD

Connect with the Author

Twitter: @warrenofwinter

Instagram: @warrenofwinter

Facebook: www.facebook.com/winterwarren

Website: www.winterwarren.com